M000211700

Babes in Gangland

THE NEW BIZARRO AUTHOR SERIES

PRESENTS

Babes in Gangland

Bix Skahill

To Stephen —
Congrats on the
big win! Spend
it wisely!

Bix Skahill
Oct 2014

Eraserhead Press
Portland, OR

ERASERHEAD PRESS
205 NE BRYANT
PORTLAND, OR 97211

WWW.ERASERHEADPRESS.COM

ISBN: 978-1-62105-125-1

Copyright © 2013 by Bix Skahill

Cover illustration created by Scott Spinks
Cover Art Copyright © 2013 by Scott Spinks

All rights reserved. No part of this book may be reproduced or
transmitted in any form or by any means, electronic or mechanical,
including photocopying, recording, or by any information storage and
retrieval system, without the written consent of the publisher, except
where permitted by law.

Printed in the USA.

Editor's Note:

Welcome to the New Bizarro Author Series. This is Bix Skahill's first book. I'm a fan of crime fiction and this book serves as a great example. I'm really into Richard Stark's Parker novels, which are dead serious. Unlike those books, *Babes in Gangland* is a comedy. Richard Stark had another series about a thief named John Dortmunder. "Richard Stark" was a pen name and the author wrote his Dortmunder books under his real name: Donald E. Westlake. While Parker might be the greatest thief who has ever "lived," Dortumunder is his complete opposite: a giant fuckup. And instead of serious shit, his books are comedies. Or at least they're supposed to be. I read the first one, thinking it was going to be the best thing ever, and I didn't even crack a smile once. So what I'm getting at is that reading *Babes in Gangland* gave me something that the Dortumunder novel failed to provide: a book of hilarious crime fiction.

Now let's talk about the series: it's designed to test the waters for new bizarro authors to see if they have what it takes to find a readership. It's up to you as far as whether or not Eraserhead Press will be publishing more of Bix's books in the future. To succeed, he must sell several hundred copies of this book over the next year. So if you like this book, I encourage you to tell your friends about it and write a review (particularly for Amazon).

Thanks so much for giving this book a chance. I hope you enjoy it as much as I enjoyed editing it.

~~Bradley Sands

To Mary, as promised. Emily, for obvious reasons
And Keith, for turning me on to the whole thing.

Chapter One

It Was a Dark and Stormy Night

Lightning overhead. Licks and licks of it. Brightening everything for a moment, then leaving the world darker than before. And rain. Enough water to wash away this whole damn town, which would have suited Ram Bountybar just fine, as he'd lost everything anyway.

Across the parking lot of Marrowburg General Hospital and Tanning Salon, Ram rushed, his head ducked. Afraid of the storm, afraid of everything, still shaking.

Once inside the safety of the emergency room, Ram realized it wasn't just the rain wetting his face—he was crying. Wiping away the tears, more came. He tried to remember the last time he'd sobbed like that but couldn't recall. Maybe when the cancer finally beat his mother, but that was many years ago, back when he was just a kid.

Now he was a grown man. An overgrown man, actually. Six and a half feet tall, clocking in at over three hundred pounds. Muscle turning to fat as he left the football field further and further behind him.

The emergency room was packed like it always was in Marrowburg. All the cracked plastic chairs were occupied and some of the wounded stood. It was SRO for the SOL.

At the far end of the emergency room, Ram recognized some of the buxom, scantily clad ladies from Stripping Through History. They were uninjured, just waiting to get their tan on. Though he'd seen their jangling mammaries on several occasions, Ram didn't acknowledge the strippers as he was on focused on his mission.

Above the crowd, thunder rumbled, shook the hospital/ tanning salon, and, for a moment, the power faltered. The

9

lights flickered and everyone in the place gasped and cried out for their savior: the Sweet Baby Geezie. It felt as if the whole world were coming apart at the seams.

Certainly Ram's life had come undone.

The lights returned and everyone breathed a sigh of relief, returning to their silent suffering.

Taking off his hat, Ram attempted to make himself smaller as he threaded through the misery. The broken bones, the blood, the crying. Not that he took note of any of it; he had problems of his own.

When the big man arrived at the check-in desk, the receptionist looked up, perturbed. She was tired, her eyes drooping. "Yes?"

"I got a call...."

"Yes...."

"About Kid Phoenix. He got... shot." The last word caught in Ram's throat.

Sleepily, the receptionist started slowly shuffling a stack of papers. "Is Kid Phoenix his real name? Cause if it ain't, I can't help you."

Ram had no idea. He'd always just called him "Kid." Everyone did. "Come on, lady, you know Kid Phoenix. Everyone in Marrowburg knows him."

Suspending her search, she asked, "Are you family?"

"Kind of. Kid and me go way back. We work together. He found me back at City Tech, when I was on the football team. Got me to throw a few games. He really cleaned up, money-wise. Unfortunately, I got caught and was asked to leave the program. Feeling sorry for me, Kid gave me a job."

Ram realized that he was talking too much, giving out too much information. Usually it was Kid's job to tell him to shut up.

"Listen, sir, I'm sorry, but if you're not family, I cannot release any information."

He was afraid she'd say that. But he was prepared, as he always was, for any obstacle. Dragging back his jacket, he revealed his holstered .44 to the receptionist.

Straightening up, she looked into his eyes and saw what he wanted her to see: nothing but glint. Putting her hand to her throat, she said, "He's down that hall, but they'll be moving him to surgery soon."

Another cough of thunder jostled the building.

Thanking the receptionist, and feeling a little bad about the gun, Ram hurried down the hall.

A door ahead of him crashed open. An army of people were inside, all gathered around a gurney as if they were at Sunday supper. But it wasn't a meal they were clamoring about; it was Kid Phoenix, who lay prone, still.

It was the first good look Ram had gotten of his boss since the shooting. It wasn't pretty.

The gangster was still dressed in his favorite suit, the white one, but now it was brown with blood and had been ripped to shreds by the doctors. Kid's face was slack, white. His mouth was open like he was screaming something, but nothing came out but the occasional ragged breath.

He was still alive, but barely.

Ram blanched, reached for the wall to steady himself.

Lightning struck what felt like only feet away, sounding like a thousand kneecaps breaking.

"Oh Sweet Baby Geezie, get me and this baby to the birthing room now!" a woman cried out behind Ram.

He turned, looked down the hall. Coming toward them, at breakneck speed, was another gurney. Atop it was a large woman who appeared to be roughly fifty months pregnant. A team of doctors and nurses were rushing her toward the maternity wing. There was no way that baby was going to sit still for much longer.

"I ain't gonna make it!"

The pregnant lady's entire medical staff was working on her, holding her down, trying to get her to breathe, mopping sweat from her brow.

Glancing back toward Kid's doctors, Ram saw that all of them were focused on Kid, their hands red with his blood.

Ram saw what, apparently, no one else saw. The two gurneys were on the same path and there was no way to avoid an awful crash. The big man considered calling out but knew it was too late.

Just as the two gurneys collided, lightning punched the hospital/tanning salon with all of its celestial might. Everything shook and shuddered and went dark, with the only light coming from sparkling crystals of blue electricity that danced upon anything metal.

In the darkness, Kid cried out. It was horrible, the sound of a body giving up its soul. For a second: silence. Ram wanted to live in that moment—it was nice and quiet, but not built to last. The pregnant woman also cried out, the terrible sound of a soul leaving a body. There was more silence as the darkness held its ground.

The next sound that pierced the abyss was the sound of a baby crying.

Chapter Two

Baby's First Words

He woke, crapped, and cried. That's what babies tend to do.

Lying in his crib, Baby Jaydon watched—through teary eyes—the giraffe mobile twirl above his head as he thought of killing his mother. Maybe fucking her first.

That's not what babies tend to do. Usually.

But Jaydon McAlister was no usual baby.

The overhead light flicked on; Mother stood in the doorway. Though she looked tired and pissed, she was still a babe. Her frumpy robe couldn't disguise her lithe body, every inch spray-tanned and gym-toned, with bushels of disheveled dishwater blonde hair and big blue eyes, bloodshot.

Slapping on a fake smile, she strode toward the crib. "Oh, Jaydon, you're up before the sun, yet again. And, of course, you're crying."

He wanted to tell her to go to hell, that when he chose to wake and crap was his own damn business, but since Jaydon had yet to master the intricacies of the English language, he remained mute.

Mother scooped Jaydon up, held him. But not too close. She studied her son: his thick black hair (which appeared to be slicked back with oil, though that was impossible), his perpetual five o'clock shadow (a condition called *lanugo*, which the pediatrician had promised for months would go away "any day now"), and the birthmark on his little shoulder, which looked exactly like a naked woman with I (HEART) SNATCH scrawled below her preposterously large breasts (which the pediatrician couldn't explain away with any amount of Latin).

Mother's nostrils flared and she shied away. "Oh, I think somebody made a horsy in their pants."

Scrunching up his baby face and surprising them both, Jaydon shouted, his voice gruff as if he'd consumed carton upon carton of cigarettes *in utero*, "Listen, bitch, they're not 'horsies.' They're turds, plain and simple!"

The world, even the giraffe mobile, stopped spinning. As if she'd been slapped, Mother glared at her child. Her jaw slack, her eyes wild.

"Hey," chirped Father from the doorway, his voice clogged with sleep and pride, "baby's first words."

"Shut up, Phil," said Mother, not even bothering to look over her shoulder. She had eyes only for her baby. Eyes like fists. "What the fuck did you just say to me, Baby Jaydon?"

"Hey now, there's no need for swears," said Father, but, per usual, no one was listening to him.

"I was just saying that 'horsies' is a stupid name for shit. And as long as I'm at the complaints window, how come I don't get no tit? When the other kiddies at the playground get hungry, their Mommies whip out their funbags. But not you. From you, I get the bottle like I'm some fucking nobody or something. C'mon, lady, let me get to second base."

Mother more or less threw Jaydon back into the crib. Landing badly, he began crying again. Pushing past her husband, crying herself, Mother hustled from the room. Through his tears, Jaydon watched her perfect ass tick tock.

Father appeared disoriented, confused. This was not a new look for him. He kept glancing back and forth between his kid and the bedroom down the hallway, where his wife had disappeared. Licking his lips, he said, "I better, uh... yeah...."

And he left Jaydon crying.

Later that morning, Jaydon woke again. Time had passed and sunlight filled the room. He felt that his early morning horsy had hardened and was now caked to the soft skin of his ass. He was considering crying out when he overheard his parents arguing in the bathroom across the hall. The bathroom is where Mother always threw her best tantrums. She was always running the tub full of steaming water, a bottle of chilled rosé on the lip. Lying there for hours, pruning her skin, getting sloshed, demanding attention.

His parents spoke in hushed, serious tones.

"Listen," hissed his father, "I wasn't the one who wanted to adopt. I said we'd be perfectly happy without a kid."

So he was adopted! Now everything made sense. That's why his parents were both blonde and fair and he was swarthy and smelled of aftershave. That's why he didn't get the funbags.

Mother laughed unevenly, drunk. "Oh, Phil, nothing could make us happy."

"There's no need to get nasty, Sydney."

"I disagree. This is nasty business. We need to send that kid back to the county or, even better, sell him to a freak show where he belongs."

For comfort, Jaydon turned to his only real friend in this world: a purple stuffed animal named Berry Bear. Held him close.

Hissing with more force, Father said, "Even though he doesn't wear one, that's hitting below the belt."

"Phil, I shave that freak twice a day and he still has a beard. He's like a common stevedore. We have to get rid of him."

"You know as well as I do there's no backsies in adoption."

Growling, Mother slid beneath the waves, signaling that the conversation was over.

Much later, Jaydon woke again to find Father standing over him, changing his dirty diaper, which now weighed about ten pounds.

The baby said, "So I'm adopted. That's no big surprise, huh? So what can you tell me about my real folks? Where am I from?"

"I don't... I don't know much. Your mother died during childbirth and no one knew who your father was."

For the first time that morning, Jaydon smiled. It was crooked. "I'm a bastard. That makes sense, right? So why did you twos adopt?"

Hanging his head a little, Father, "The Sweet Baby Geezie didn't see fit to put my seed in your mother."

"That's a sad story. Let me guess... you wanted to keep trying, but Mommie Dearest was sick of you hiding your salami in her lunch pail, ain't that so?"

"That's not exactly—"

"And now that she has a kid, I bet she don't even let *you* get to second base."

Frowning, Father, "Don't talk about your mother like that."

"What? She can't hear me, she's too drunk. Besides, you just told me she ain't my real mother."

"Now she's your real mother, and I'm your real father, and to show the world what a happy little family we are, we're going to Dead Cow Burger Joint for lunch."

Chapter Three

Fucking Dead Cow Burger

Father strapped Jaydon into his car seat in the back of the mini-van while Mother poured herself into the passenger seat. The baby looked around at his neighborhood, a frown blossoming on his chubby cheeks.

The McAlisters lived in a suburb of Marrowburg called Hide Park where all the houses looked more or less the same and were all painted taupe, sandstone, or dusty dust. The lawns were all manicured, everyone owned matching birdbaths, and every family had a just-washed minivan parked in their driveway.

One could barely smell the pungent aroma of the many slaughterhouses that called Marrowburg home.

"Jesus," said Jaydon, "what a character-less shithole. I mean, if you came home drunk, how would you know which house was yours?"

Her head in her hands, Mother said, "Why don't you shut the hell up, Baby Jaydon?"

"What? For months, you've been trying to get me to talk, now you want me to zip it?"

"I was trying to get you to say 'Mama' or 'Papa,' not to swear like a common stevedore."

Getting behind the wheel, Father said, "Listen, family, we're going to Dead Cow Burger Joint for lunch, where we're going to have a normal fast food eating experience like normal families. Does everyone understand?"

"I want you to shut the hell up too, Phil."

"This is a real fucking treat, you know it," said Jaydon, who'd never eaten at Dead Cow Burger Joint before. The

McAlisters hadn't even gotten their food yet; they were just standing in a long line. Everyone loved Dead Cow Burger Joint.

"Be still, you little ass," hissed Mother, who held her son tenuously, as if he were a ticking time bomb.

"I want a Dead Cow Kiddie Banquet Box," Jaydon said, louder this time, trying to draw attention. Not that he got it. The talking baby with slicked back hair, whiskers, and a potty mouth drew only a few cursory glances; this was Marrowburg where freaks were a dime a dozen, *literally*, at Freaks R Us.

Softly, Mother warned, "Stop your fucking swearing or I'll drop you so hard."

As much as he could, the baby tried to shy away from his mother. "Sweet Baby Geezie, you're one crazy bitch, you know that? And to boot you smell like a fucking brewery exploded in your mouth." He turned his bald, bulbous head and addressed the crowd, "Hey, nobody smoke around this bitch. She's about 90 proof."

With a grunt, Mother pulled Jaydon close to her chest, pressing his little face into her bosom to silence him.

Finally getting some tit, thought the baby with some satisfaction.

Putting a light hand on his wife's back, Father said, "Okay, everyone, let's remain calm. Now, Jaydon, you only have two teeth. If you tried to eat a hamburger, you'd choke."

Pulling his head back, Jaydon forsook the tit. "I'll take my chances. I want a fucking Dead Cow Kiddie Banquet Box. I need a little fucking protein. You want me to be big and strong like you, don't ya, Daddy?"

These words visibly stung Father, who had arms like matchsticks and stood a good three inches shorter than his wife.

Trying to remain calm, like all the baby books advised, Father turned away from his son, started counting. Everyone remained quiet until it was their turn to order. Father, his voice frail but full of defiance, said, "The wife and I will have two Dead Cow Meals and a small fry for the kid."

"Maybe you didn't hear me so good, Daddy, but I want a fucking Dead Cow Kiddie Banquet Box complete with a hamburger and some shitty Chink toy!"

Leaning into her husband, Mother whispered, "Let me drop him, Phil, please. If he lands just right on his little soft fontanel, this nightmare will be over."

"Sweet Baby Geezie, I'd recognize that fucking voice anywhere!" These words erupted from the guy working behind the counter and were said loud enough to turn heads throughout the fast food restaurant. He pointed a finger, thick and greasy. "I know that kid."

Slowly, as he was still developing his neck muscles, Jaydon turned toward the Dead Cow Burger Joint employee. The guy was middle-aged but bulky, six and a half feet of muscle buried beneath layers of fat. Bald and dull-eyed. His mouth hung open, which seemed to be its natural state.

When their eyes met, it was as if flavored fireworks went off inside Jaydon's soft head. He knew this person, although in his nine months of existence he'd never laid eyes on him. His feelings toward this mountain of a man were warm; they were friends. Sometime in the past. They'd bowled together, drank together, chased the same tail.

But that's impossible, Jaydon thought. He couldn't bowl; he'd only recently been able to pull himself to his feet on low tables. Which also made chasing tail something of a chore.

The baby didn't have time to dwell on this inconsistency, as a new, unpleasant sensation filled him. Flashes of images invaded his tiny baby mind: *a chorus of thunder, lightning exposing the dark world around him. An alley, brick and dumpsters, puddles of greasy water. Then, from behind him, a shot. The loudest shot he'd ever heard, and he heard plenty of shots in his life. Fired most of them. And pain. Searing pain burning up his back and then... then nothing.*

Jaydon, still feeling a phantom pain racing, started bawling, kicking his pudgy legs. On swift feet, Mother rushed him away from the counter, away from his old friend whom he'd never met, away from his Dead Cow Kiddie Banquet Box.

Sprawled on the living room floor, Jaydon shook his rattle —which was shaped like a dolphin—with a vengeance, as if he were throttling someone. But even this couldn't soothe his agitated nerves.

Mother, who was just as agitated, paced in a tight circle around her child, glass of rosé in her hand. Her face an ugly mask of anger.

"What did that fat fuck behind the counter mean?" she asked. "He said he *knew* Jaydon."

Father said, "I dunno. That was weird."

"It was more than weird, Phil. It was downright creepy. I'm calling the cops, that's what I'm doing, I'll call the cops and they'll arrest that fat pervert and throw him in prison, where he'll hopefully get assfucked to death."

Jaydon knew that the guy from Dead Cow Burger Joint was no pedophile. He was a stand-up guy. The baby just didn't know how he knew that.

Tossing the rattle aside, Jaydon spoke up, "Listen, lady, you don't know shit about–"

Mother spun on him, flashed her angry eyes. "You! I want you to go back to gurgling, making horsies, and lying around looking stupid! No more of your fresh talk, young man!"

Waving his arms to signal surrender, Father made his way across the floor to talk peace. "Okay, everyone has had a very trying day. I think Mama and Baby both need a nap. We'll finish this discussion when I get home from my client meeting."

"Client meeting? Our lives are falling apart all around us and you're going to go push your stupid designs?"

"They're building a new Tommy's Cuban Cigars and Quick Abortions and I want them to use my design! I'll be back around five and we can work everything out. Now both of you should lie down and get some shut-eye. And

Sydney, I'm warning you, you are not to harm this baby in any way."

Mother watched Father gather his briefcase, her eyes daggers, her fists forming.

A bottle of rosé in one hand and a baby in the other, Mother lurched into Jaydon's room, where everything was blue and happy, but that was just decoration. She dropped Jaydon into his crib. He bounced a few times, cried out, "Hey, lady, watch the merchandize. You heard what Phil said: no hurtsies."

Mother shoved her face into Jaydon's; he feared she was going to swallow him. "Shut up, you little monster. I know what you are. You're the devil."

"Sweet Baby Geezie, where is your fucking maternal instinct? I think you need a fucking break. We should get one of them *au pairs*. Preferably a French one, with a nice *au pair* of Alps."

He was just cracking wise to cover up how scared he was. There were tears of fear in his eyes.

She slapped him, right across the face, a real wallop. He swore and started bawling in earnest. "Oh, cry all you want, you baby. That's just the beginning of your pain. Right now I'm going to take a long hot bath to calm my overwrought nerves and when I finish, I'm going to give you a nice long bath. Hold you under until your tiny monster lungs fill with water and you cease to exist."

On drunken pins, Mother stumbled from the room, laughing mirthlessly. Without thinking, Jaydon reached over and pulled Berry Bear close. He knew he was in for it, knew he was going to buy the farm, that nothing was going to save him now.

Chapter Four

With a Little Help from My Friends

For several anxious minutes, Jaydon lay in his crib listening to the tub fill. He considered crying out, calling for help, but knew the only thing he'd get would be a sore throat. All he could do was whimper. The thing that pissed him off the most about dying was that when his life flashed before his eyes, it would be short and not particularly interesting.

So concerned with his wallowing, he didn't notice the large shadow fill the doorway. He wasn't aware of the guy from Dead Cow Burger Joint until the man came forward on tentative feet, stared down into the crib with curious eyes. Said in a gruff voice, "When I first saw you, I thought you was just another bearded, talking baby, but then the things you said, the way you said them... I... I had to follow you home. I just had to find out if... if you're really him."

Like a punch of lightning, something else came back to the little tyke. This large man's name: Ram, Ram Bountybar.

"I don't know who you think I am, Ram, but you gotta get me out of this fucking cage. That bath-taking bitch is gonna kill me."

The big man's eyes went wide. "How do you know my name?"

"I don't know. That doesn't matter now. Just get me outta here."

From across the hall, Mother called, "Jaydon, are you talking to someone?"

The way her words tottered, he could tell she was completely blotto.

"No," Jaydon called back, "just crying."

"Good," she said, smug, satisfied.

22

Ram's callus-y hands carefully cradled the baby, lifted him. Jaydon could feel this man's numerous muscles tense. For the first time Jaydon felt like he might survive the afternoon. He ordered Ram to put him down on his feet.

"Can you even walk, little baby?"

"As long as I got something to hang on to."

As gently as the lummox could, Ram placed Jaydon on the floor. The baby grasped the bars of his crib, took a few faltering steps. Almost fell.

Ram reached for him. "Lemme help you."

"No, this is something I got to do myself. Hand me that baby monitor."

"The what?"

"That white thing on the dresser, you idiot, the thing that looks like a radio. And leave it plugged in."

The big man did as he was told. Jaydon clutched the antenna of the egg-shaped baby monitor in one tiny hand and clung to the crib with the other. Determined, he made his way toward the door. Leaving the crib railing, he clung to the changing table, then to the rocking chair. Finally, trundling on unsteady legs, taking his first real steps, he crossed the floor to the door.

Looking across the expanse of open space between him and the bathroom door, he turned to Ram.

"Hey, Ram, I might need a hand with this part."

Nodding, Ram thrust out his giant hand. Jaydon took it and together they made it across the hallway. Through the bathroom door, the baby could hear his skunked mother singing. He'd never heard her this happy.

The baby looked up at Ram, who towered over him. "Now open this door and let me do my thing."

Ram said, "Maybe we should just get out of here while the getting is good."

"Fuck that, open this goddamn door."

Frowning, Ram twisted the knob and melted back into the shadows of the hallway.

Mother was so drunk that, although she was looking right at him, it took her a minute to focus on Jaydon. The baby studied her, memorizing what hate looked like.

"You know, Mother, you really do have nice tits." He turned on the monitor. A red light winked.

"How'd you get out of your crib? And what are you doing with that baby monitor?"

"Father told you not to hurt me but he never said anything about the other way 'round."

"What the hell is that supposed to mean?"

"It's just too bad that your nice tits have to die along with you."

A look of miserable realization washed over her face as she suddenly sobered. "You little fuck, you wouldn't dare!"

Using every ounce of his baby strength, Jaydon hurled the baby monitor. There was just enough power cord.

Mother and baby watched the white orb sail through the air. It made a lovely arc before hitting the water with a beautiful splash.

Her large but firm breasts flopping, Mother jerked and danced. She bit her tongue. Blood flowed. A sound came out of her throat, horrible and hollow: a manic hum.

After a few moments, she stopped twitching, stopped making noise.

A smile appeared on Jaydon's face. So wide that a stalactite of drool grew down.

Jaydon attempted the return journey across the hallway without help. He made it roughly halfway, but fell on his butt. Luckily, he was well versed at landing on his ass.

Even after the baby toppled, Ram kept to the shadows. Slowly motioning toward the bathtub, the body, he asked, "Why... why did you do that?"

"I had to."

"But, but she was your mother. And she had a great rack."

"Listen, Ram. It was either her or me, so get over it. And help me get back into my room. We gotta pack some stuff and get the hell out of here before the heat arrives."

Slowly, Ram peeled himself from the darkness, offered a hand. Together, the huge man and the tiny baby toddled into Jaydon's room. Ram looked around as if they had just landed on a strange planet. "So, what do you need? That cage or the giraffe thing that goes round and round?"

"Fuck that shit. I need clothes. Onesies mostly, nothing too cute. And no sleeves, I want the world to see my awesome tattoo. Diapers and talcum powder are in the top drawer of the changing table along with some teething gel. I'm hooked on that sweet sauce. Grab some toys. I really like my dolphin rattle and anything with a mirror on it. It's always a fucking surprise when I see my fucking reflection. My binky too—that's that thing you stick in my mouth to stop me crying—it's somewhere in the crib. You got to have that shit cause sometimes I just go a little crazy and there's no controlling me. And don't forget Berry Bear. He's also in the crib. I need him to fall asleep. The darkness is scary and Berry Bear protects me from that shit."

Chapter Five

Into the Past Darkly

When they got out to Ram's car there were two surprises. First, Ram drove a lilac-colored Dodge Aspire, which seemed an odd choice for the massive man, and secondly, there was already a baby car seat installed.

When Jaydon inquired about these anomalies, Ram, throwing an overstuffed diaper bag in the lilac trunk, hemmed and hawed for a moment. "Oh, that, yeah, well, this is my sister's car, and I'm just borrowing it."

An hour later, gnawing on a fistful of Dead Cow Burger Joint French fries, Jaydon sat on a plaid blanket beneath a sprawling oak. Watched the murky water of the Rendering River slip past, chunks of chewed potato spotting his chest and stomach.

Ram sat beside him with a paper napkin tucked into his shirt, savagely tearing into his second Jumbo Dead Cow Burger. He also had food all over him.

"Okay, Ram," said the baby, spitting matriculated food, "explain to me how I know you."

"Well, I knew you when you weren't you."

Jaydon laughed sarcastically. "That don't make no sense."

"I know, none of this does." Ram took another massive bite, as if the discussion were over.

"Well, can you at least fucking try to explain?"

Shrugging, Ram said, "Okay. You used to be another guy. A guy named Kid Phoenix. We worked together in the Marrowburg underworld. You was a gangster and I was your henchman. We ran numbers, collected debts, roughed up the people who forgot to pay their protection money. Stuff like that."

26

Usually Jaydon liked to simply chew on puzzle pieces, but now he was putting them together. "Then... then I got shot... in the back... in an alley."

"Yeah, that was a sad night. It happened about nine months ago. You got gunned down behind Stripping Through History, Paulo Banko's place. When I found out, I ran to the hospital, but I was too late. You was already dying. And then there was a bunch of lightning and there was this pregnant lady giving birth and..."

Realization dawned the horizon of Jaydon's mind. "Rein-fucking-carnation. My soul was passed into this...." He motioned down toward his chubby body and the ellipses of fry specks across his onesie, which featured a lion's head roaring.

"Yeah, I guess. It's pretty freaky."

Accepting that he had been this character Kid Phoenix and he now lived in a baby's body, Jaydon got down to business. "Okay. So who's the rat who punched my ticket?"

Another shrug, another bite. "I don't know, nobody does. Not even the coppers."

Trying to keep the anger out of his voice, he said, "You didn't try to find out?"

"After you bit the dust, I skedaddled out of town. I was scared, afraid I might be next on the hit list. Came out here to hide in Hide Park. Got a job at Dead Cow Burger Joint and, well, you know the rest."

"Great. Well, finish your fucking Dead Cow Jumbo Burger, we got work to do."

"Like what?"

"Well, first off, and I hate to ask you to do this, but you gotta change my diaper. I just laid a doozy of a fucking horsy. Then we're going back into the city and find the fuck who twitched me and we're gonna twitch him."

Leaving Hide Park in the rearview mirror, Ram aimed his lilac-colored automobile toward the heart of the city. The sun was just setting behind the skyline comprised mainly of abattoirs and whorehouses.

Holding Berry Bear tight, Jaydon fell into a deep sleep—vehicular motion always had that effect on him—and he dreamt of bloody revenge.

When he awoke the following morning, they were parked in the Marrowburg Public Library and Convenience Store parking lot and Ram was staring at him, waiting for him to wake.

"I got a bad feeling about this, boss. Nine months ago someone wanted you dead and now you're going back, poking around. And no offense, but you seem pretty defenseless, being a baby and all."

"True, but I got you... don't I?"

"Sure, sure you do. But just think, you and me could light out somewhere. I could raise you, be your dad or whatever. I could find another Dead Cow Burger Joint, in another suburb, and–"

"Just drive, Ram, and stop thinking. Take me to the place where I got plugged."

Chapter Six

Watching Helen Keller Take Off Her Clothes

When they pulled up outside Stripping Through History, a fist of memories punched Jaydon right in his tiny baby face: holding court at the strip club's bar, doing his best to deplete the nation's whiskey supply, slapping pretty girls on the ass while stuffing dollar bills into their skimpy period costumes.

Staring at the neon sign out front, which featured a naked female with her nose in a book (titled *Stripping Through History*) that was wedged between her voluminous breasts, Jaydon said, "This is where I used to hang out."

Ram laughed, just a touch. "Yeah, you didn't care much for the history learning. You was only here because of Ruby Redd."

Ruby Redd. Those two words hit Jaydon right in his balls, which had yet to drop. He visualized a woman: statuesque, pale, flaming red hair flowing down her back like strands of lava. Possessing curves that only a German could design. Full lips that were always curved upwards into something that wasn't quite a smile. Emerald eyes that flashed when she was happy, more when she was angry.

"She was my gal, wasn't she, Ram?"

"*Was*, yeah. She worked here, stripping as Amelia Earhart. In her act, the last article of clothing she'd remove was her aviator goggles. That really drove the old men crazy."

Jaydon could picture Ruby Redd onstage, beneath the colored lights, wearing nothing by a leather helmet and goggles, her mouth running a mile a minute about pioneering females in the male-dominated world of flight. Thinking of her large breasts swaying made the baby thirsty. "Let's go in."

"Gee, boss, do you think that's a good idea?'

He turned on his henchman, his eyes dancing with rage. "Why not?"

"Well, for one thing, I'm pretty sure there's an age limit."

Spitting and shaking his dolphin rattle, Jaydon, "I don't give a flying fuck about no age limit. I gotta talk with Paulo."

Although the baby didn't voice it, they both knew that the baby was hoping to catch a glimpse of Ruby Redd and her magnificent funbags.

With a resigned sigh, Ram grabbed the diaper bag, hoisted the baby from his car seat, and headed toward the club.

On the walk, Jaydon spotted a ragged political poster stapled to a light pole. It was for Senator Dove and featured his catchphrase: *Never Indicted!* This poster brought another memory careening back: Ruby Redd loved this Senator Dove, even campaigned for him. Kid thought this was a waste of time, as he hated all politicians, but there was something about this Senator Dove that drove him particularly crazy. Maybe it was because this politician didn't have any balls. Literally. His entire nutsack had been been blown off in the heat of battle. Or maybe it was the way Ruby Redd gushed over him and wouldn't shut up about him.

That dame sure was crazy, he thought as they stepped into the club.

Walking through the door of Stripping Through History was like being swallowed. Outside, despite the smog and general slaughterhouse fug of Marrowburg, the day was sunny. Inside the club, it was darker than a month of nights. And loud. Noise everywhere: thumping bass, the clinking of ice, the hooting of desperate men.

In the back was a small stage. Upon said stage: a tiny woman wearing a tight bodice that pushed her breasts so far north Admiral Byrd would have never found them. She was also wearing sunglasses. Her arms out before her, she stumbled around, bumping into the stripper pole.

"Oh that poor lady," observed Ram, "she's blind."

"Wa... ter... Wa... ter," cried the woman from the stage haltingly.

Ram, shaking his head, "Oh no, and she's also deaf."

"Sweet Baby Geezie, you idiot, she's only pretending to be deaf and blind. She's Helen Keller."

As if suddenly bestowed the gift of sight, she ripped off her bodice and flung it into the crowd of horny wolves. They cheered. One shouted, "Show us your miracle-worker!"

Although he wanted to see how the act ended, Jaydon suddenly had to close his eyes due to the pain flaring in his skull. It was coming back to him: the night he got killed. In drips and drabs. He remembered having a heated argument with Paulo in the back office right before he walked out into the storm and got plugged. Jaydon searched his baby mind, but could not recall the subject of the disagreement.

He commanded Ram to take him back to Paulo's office. "Make sure we're not seen."

Although Jaydon stood out like a baby in a strip club, Ram made it to the back of the club without being seen by sticking to the copious shadows of Stripping Through History. When they reached the office door, which was down a short dark hall at the back of the club, Ram faltered. There was a colony of sweat beneath his nose. "You know, boss, once we go through this door, there ain't no going back. You and me, we could just walk away right now and I could raise you and we could both be happy."

"Fuck that domestic shit! We're talking to Paulo!"

Ram formed a resigned fist. Jaydon spat, shaking his rattle heatedly, "No, you fool, kick the door in. This is a surprise party for Paulo. We don't want to send him an invite."

Rearing back, Ram did as he was told. The deafening sound of splintering wood and wrenched hinges filled the world. Jaydon wanted to cover his ears but he lacked the motor control.

Paulo, a thick man with thin hair, was behind his desk. He sprung to his feet, upsetting the meal he was consuming. It was some kind of fast-food Mexican feast: ground beef, beans, and cheese. Fattening, greasy. There were stains on his shirt and it was hard to tell if they were new or old.

The club owner bent, with great difficulty, to retrieve something from the bottom drawer of his desk. Most likely a weapon. But he stopped when he saw Ram. Though a hesitant smile spread across Paulo's face, it took him a moment to find the lid to his voice box. "Hey, Ram... when did you have a kid?"

"He didn't. It's me."

When Paulo's bulging eyes settled on the I (HEART) SNATCH tattoo on the baby's shoulder, his semi-smile died on the vine. Flicking his lizard tongue, he wetted his lips as if he were being paid by the lick. "Kid... but... but I saw your body."

"I got a new model. I'm a fucking reincarnation, Paulo. What do you think 'bout that? I'm back from the dead and I'm as mad as hell and I'm gonna find the dickface who killed me. The scene of the crime seemed the logical place to start. So, the night I was plugged, you and me was in this very room arguing about something."

Paulo tried to laugh but nothing came out. Sweat broke out on his jowly face. Or that could have just been grease. "It... that weren't nothing, Kid. Just a little disagreement between two friends."

"What was it about? Money."

"No, no, nothing that serious. It was about dames. Well, one dame in particular."

"Ruby Redd? We was fighting over Ruby Redd?"

"It wasn't *over* her, Kid. And like I said, it wasn't no fight. It was more of a discussion between friends. Ruby Redd had broken it off with you. She wanted to start a new life, get out of the stripping and history business, and have a family. Knowing you didn't want that, she... well, she dumped you. You were sure there was another guy in the picture, so you came to me to see if I had any information on the subject, which I didn't. So you see, you was really mad at Ruby Redd, not me."

These injurious words made Jaydon's tiny heart, which was already palpitating like a hummingbird's, beat even faster. It came back to him: that final fight with Ruby Redd, her stomping out of Jimmy Doyle's Café and Oil Change, his certainty that she was getting some strange on the side.

Unable to control his rage, Jaydon began to wail. "Give me the fucking binky, Ram. I'm fucking losing it!"

With his sausage-y fingers, the goon dug around in the diaper bag, frantic and clumsy. Finally he found the binky, waved it around as if it were a white flag. "Whadda I do? Whadda I do?"

"Stick it in my fucking mouth, you idiot!"

Ram rammed the pacifier in the baby's mouth. The crying ended instantly. For a moment the only sounds in the office were the sound of sucking and Paulo trying to breathe right.

Ripping the binky from his mouth, Jaydon tossed it indifferently to the floor. "After we're done here, Ram, boil that shit in hot water. Now you..." The baby pointed at the strip club owner with his dolphin rattle and said, "Okay, where is Ruby Redd now?"

"I don't... I don't got no idea, Kid. After that night, you know, the night you passed away, I ain't never seen her again. She moved, changed her number, disappeared off the face of the earth."

"Okay, great, that's fucking awesome. So let's get back to the night in question. While we was fighting or discussing or whatever, you got called to the front of the club. When you came back, you had a message that I was to meet someone out in the alley. Who gave you that message?"

"Rinky Dink."

Rinky Dink's horribly burned face swam before Jaydon's brain. The baby thought: *what an ugly fuck.*

When he was young, Rinky Dink broke into a potato chip factory on a dare and, unfortunately, fell into a vat of boiling oil. This scarred him for life in two ways: his face looked like a topographical map of hell and he always smelled slightly of chive and onion. Unable to land a normal job thanks to his ruined visage and unusual scent, Rinky Dink sought out a life of crime. But even in the vast Marrowburgian underworld he was a bottom-feeder. He didn't work for any gang in particular. Just did trivial work for whoever had the money:

running messages, stealing license plates, entertaining at Halloween parties.

Jaydon knew Rinky Dink wasn't the guy who plugged him. He didn't have the initiative or the balls; Jaydon had never even seen him with a gun. The gangster baby asked, "Who sent Rinky Dink?"

Shaking and sweating, Paulo said, "I ain't got no idea. Rinky Dink just told me the message, not who it was from."

"Then you ain't got any more information for me."

"No, I guess I don't," said Paulo, relieved that this interview was drawing to a close.

"Alright, then you've exhausted your usefulness. Ram, kill him."

"Ah Geez, boss, really?"

His face reddening, Jaydon squealed, "Yes, really. And here, use this." The baby held out the dolphin rattle. "Ram it down his throat, Ram."

Paulo shrank all the way down to the floor, a lump of fear. "Why, Kid? Why do you gotta kill me?"

"Cause I'm feeling colicky."

The giant henchman gently placed the baby on the floor with his back against a chair. The rattle shaking, Ram advanced on the cowering Paulo. As if it would do any good, Paulo held his hands above his head. He wasn't going to stop Ram. Nothing stopped him when he got going.

Pulling on Paulo's greasy hair, Ram made the strip club owner face him. There were tears in Paulo's eyes. He trembled with fear. This made Jaydon so happy he kicked his little legs uncontrollably.

With one neat thrust, Ram rammed the dolphin rattle into Paulo's mouth all the way to the hilt. Choking, Paulo kicked and flopped. Little good that did him. Ram held his ground, shoving the rattle deeper and deeper.

Two sounds filled the office: a man choking to death and a baby giggling.

Chapter Seven

Dating an Old Man

As he strapped Jaydon into the back of the lilac Dodge Aspire and police sirens disturbed the peace in the distance, Ram asked the baby, "So, I guess we're gonna go after poor Rinky Dink now, huh?"

"I was thinking of a different fish, a fish with bigger tits. Ruby Redd."

The big man blanched, stopped strapping. "But... but you heard what Paulo said. She's disappeared off the face of the earth."

"She's still in Marrowburg. I can feel it in my bones."

"I ain't gonna stick a rattle down no lady's throat."

"That ain't gonna happen, Ram, I'm fresh out of rattles. C'mon, you know me, I ain't gonna hurt Ruby Redd. She's the love of my life. Besides, she obviously ties into my death. Whoever she dumped me for is the guy who twisted me."

"Well, yeah, maybe. But remember, boss, you had plenty of enemies."

"Thanks for the reminder. Now, let's find Ruby Redd. We'll start with Violet Greene."

Jaydon would never admit that he really just wanted to see Ruby Redd, needed to see her. Not that he held any illusions about his chances of winning her back in his current state. She could never love a man who was only twenty-eight inches long, couldn't achieve an erection, and still crapped in his pants. It would be like dating an old man.

Chapter Eight

Officer Bertrand Kropp Gets His 1,455th Partner

Officer Bertrand Kropp's fellow assholes-in-blue had gone through the trouble of putting a hundred candles on his cake. This pissed him off and made the flaming confection before him look more like a bonfire than a dessert. He knew the other cops were simply mocking him and his advanced age. No one liked him at Precinct 13. Not his fellow officers, not the Captain, not even the janitors who refused to dispose of his soiled Depends.

Though a great majority of his fellow officers considered him an old fool, Bertrand saw himself as the Sweet Baby Geezie's gift to copdom. This belief led him to remain on the force well after the required retirement age. Through his seventies, eighties, and nineties, Bertrand still considered himself viable. Even with his Parkinson's and glaucoma and mild dementia and shitty sciatica and bladder control issues, he was a damn fine cop. At least in his book.

Until now.

As he approached his 100th birthday, Bertrand had come to a realization: now that he had inoperable lung cancer, failing kidneys, and an irremovable tumor in his brain the size of a Shih Tzu, it was finally time to hang up his gun, take off his badge. Or, more precisely, have someone else take off the badge since he couldn't really control his hands.

After today, his 100th birthday, he was finally retiring.

As a last slap in his wrinkly face, the other cops—who were obviously jealous of his gift of second sight, which nearly helped him apprehend criminals—gathered with their smug smiles for a combined birthday and retirement party complete with a flaming cake and several boxes of Depends with colorful bows affixed.

But he'd show them. He was going to extinguish every single one of those candles, even if it took him all afternoon. Even if it was the last thing he did in his career as a cop. He was gonna go out with a bang.

As he was drawing in as much breath as his ancient lungs could hold, the phone on a nearby desk clattered. Everyone looked at it like it was a fart.

"Sweet Baby Geezie," bellowed Captain Milktwat, "I thought I told you penis-less fucks to take all the phones off the hook so we could give this asshole a proper send off."

All the cops, ashamed, looked down. The phone continued its journey through Ringland.

Tired of holding his breath, Bertrand breathed out, said, "Maybe someone should answer that."

All the cops looked at one another. No one wanted to answer the phone; there was never any good news coming into police headquarters.

Cap screamed, "Hey, Globule, you answer it!"

Officer Globule shrugged, said, "I would, Cap, but my rosacea is pretty bad."

"Okay, alright. Hinders, you get the phone."

"My rosacea is flaring up too."

Captain Milktwat looked around at his men. All of them were suffering from outbreaks of rosacea, their faces red, puffy. It was quite disgusting, really. Cap's eyes settled on an unblemished but wrinkly face standing at the back of the squad room. He pointed.

"You, rookie, you get the phone."

"Me?" squeaked the surprised young man. "But I'm not, I'm not really an officer of the law."

"Yeah, Cap," explained Hinders, "that's the dying kid, the one from Dream Comers, that organization that gives terminal kids a chance to do something fun right before they kick the bucket."

Captain Milktwat narrowed his eyes at the person in question. He was stooped, had a bald head, and wrinkly skin. Using all his detecting skills, Cap said, "You don't look like no kid."

Clearing his throat, the dying kid, "I suffer from Progeria, an aging disease. Though I'm thirteen, I look like I'm eighty."

"That sucks. Do you have rosacea?"

"Ah, no."

"Well that's a silver lining, huh? So, son, what's your name?"

"I'm Officer-For-A-Day Thimbleton."

"Well, Officer-For-A-Day Thimbleton, answer that phone."

"But... but I'm not really a police officer, I–"

Captain Milktwat erupted, "Listen, if you're in uniform and in my squad room, you're on my force. Now pick up that phone, you shirking son-of-a-bitch!"

Shaking, Thimbleton made his way through the men in blue with bad skin. He answered the phone. A short conversation ensued.

During that time, no one noticed that Bertrand was desperately, and quite unsuccessfully, attempting to blow out his hundred candles. Everyone was watching the dying kid on the phone. Watching his face fall as he took down some information.

Finally, he hung up the phone and looked around the room, which looked back at him.

After a deep sigh, his voice clogged with forlornness, Thimbleton admitted there'd been yet another murder in the city limits.

"That's not surprising," laughed Globule, "this being Marrowburg and all."

"Who was it this time? And please tell me it was a politician," said another cop whose name no one ever got right.

Thimbleton shook his head. "Paulo Banko, the owner of Stripping Through History."

Heated swearing flooded the squad room. Striping Through History was one of the cops' favorite places to hang out. Paulo had always been kind to them: members of the Marrowburg police force received free person history lessons and lap dances.

"What kind of sick fuck would kill Paulo?" asked Officer Hinders.

"That's our job to find that out, boys. Dying kid, this is now your case."

"But... but... that isn't what Dream Comers is all about."

"Well, you should have thought of that before you answered that phone."

"But I'm, I'm not really an officer of the law," Thimbleton reiterated.

"You're wearing a badge, aren't you?"

The dying kid fingered the plastic badge on his pigeon chest. "Not really. These are a pair of wings a pilot gave me on my last flight."

"Good enough for me. You and Officer Globule take a patrol cart down to Striping Through History and find out what's what."

Bertrand had given up on trying to blow out his candles as his chest ached. At first, he thought it was yet another stroke. The irony of the fact that he might die on his last day on the force was not lost on him. But then his head began to spin and his brain cringed. This wasn't a stroke; it was something different, something better. It was his Gift, his second sight: in his mind, Bertrand could see a black man shooting Paulo Banko in the chest on some sandy beach.

He sat up as straight as he could with his sciatica flaring. "Cap, you gotta send me out on this one."

Everyone looked at Bertrand, having nearly forgotten his existence. Milktwat screamed, "What are you talking about, you worthless old coot? You're retired!"

"Not for..." Bertrand lifted his hand very, very, very slowly. Squinted at his watch "... another six hours."

Cap shook his head, disturbing his rosacea. "No way. Dying boy, take Globule and get going."

"Wait!" screamed Bertrand. With great difficulty, Bertrand nearly stood, his back as crooked as a crook. Knees popping, groaning. "My second sight is kicking in, Cap. I gotta be on this case."

Every cop in the room groaned.

"You do realize," Captain Milktwat pointed out, "that you've been on the force for eight-four years and you've never solved a single case, with or without your supposed gift. The last time you had one of your fucking visions, we found you three days later, wandering out in the country, naked and smeared with chewed licorice."

Looking down with his glaucoma-y eyes, the ancient cop mumbled, "I took a wrong turn on Cracklings Drive."

The cops burst out in laughter.

"Now Thimbleton, get your dying ass out of here and–"

"Wait," yelled Bertrand. Taking his sweet time, he reached beneath his suit coat and pulled out a gun. Gripping it by the barrel he pointed it in the general direction of Captain Milktwat.

Tossing his hands in the air like confetti, Cap screamed, "Have you lost your mind, Kropp?"

"Perhaps. You're right, in over eighty years, I haven't solved a single case. I'm still an Officer Third Class, still walk a beat when my rheumatism isn't bad, and I'm well aware that my second sight is considered to be some kind of joke, but now is my time to shine. I can feel it, I'm going out with a bang."

For a moment, Captain Milktwat studied the old man. Shook his head. "Alright, have it your way. This is your baby, Officer-For-A-Day Thimbleton and Officer Kropp. Make sure it isn't a stillbirth."

"Thanks, Cap."

Bertrand shuffled toward the door and the young man who looked old followed in his wake. It took them a good five minutes to clear the room.

"Well," said Captain Milktwat, "with any luck, both of those fucks will be dead by sundown."

The assembled cops laughed. They were so busy chuckling, slapping each other on their cop backs, and comparing rosacea scars that no one noticed Officer Globule backing too close to the cake and going up in flames.

Down the garage, Bertrand struggled getting into the police cart. It was quite a chore getting his old body onto the buckboard and he groaned with every movement.

Officer-For-A-Day Thimbleton stood beneath him, ready to break his fall. "Ah, hey, Mr. Kropp, do you need a hand?"

"Not from you, fuckface."

"Excuse me?"

"Listen, you know we've never gotten along, probably stemming from that time that I accidentally tripped you with my cane when we failed to catch the Marrowburg Strangler."

"I think... I think you might be mistaking me for someone else. I'm new around here, I'm the dying boy."

Reaching the buckboard, Bertrand sat, bones cracking. He turned to look down at Thimbleton, squinted. "You can cut the lip anytime, boy. It's a simple mistake to make. All you rookies look the same to me."

"Ah, yeah, about that. I don't know if you heard up in the squad room, but I'm not really a cop. I'm just, well, I'm just visiting."

Bertrand hadn't heard and he didn't hear now. His ears hadn't truly functioned in decades. "Great, whatever. We're partners now and we'll try to put all past grievances behind us. Now, get up here. You should drive. I can't really see the horse, much less the road."

Chapter Nine

Ape Priest

Violet Greene was Ruby Redd's best friend. Ironically, they were as different as could be. While Ruby Redd was tall and beautiful, Violet was short, swarthy, and looked as if she did her grooming with a rake.

But the two women were inseparable. When Ruby Redd first arrived in town from some shit farm out in the sticks, everyone treated her cruelly by shoving her, tripping her, making fun of the fact that she didn't smell like dead animals (which is referred to as "the Marrowburg welcome"). Violet was the first ray of light she experienced in the big city. She took her in, rarely mocked her fresh scent, and helped her get a job at Stripping Through History. While Ruby Redd danced as the ethereal, faux Amelia Earhart, Violet was the earthy, ersatz Bella Abzug.

The two women were inseparable. If anyone knew where Ruby Redd was holding up, it was Violet Greene, who lived in the Gelatin District.

In a city where several neighborhoods vied for "most dangerous," the Gelatin District had a pretty good claim to the title. The skyline was comprised of mostly deserted, burned-out shells of buildings, graffiti—incorporating a two-pronged attack of poor grammar and atrocious spelling—covered every available surface, and the populace was made up mostly of forgers, pickpockets, and jaywalkers. Also, it was the home of the Marrowburg Zoo and Unobservatory (the telescope had been pilfered years ago), a facility with famously lax security. Not a sweltering summer would go by without some kid getting devoured or mauled by some horrible beast. Just the previous winter, it had been discovered that the priest at St. Jude's Catholic Church and Off-Track Betting was actually a gorilla who'd escaped his confines over eight years before.

As the lilac Aspire dodged its way through the Gelatin District—down Beef Marrow Boulevard, which was lousy with potholes and jaywalkers—Ram stepped on the gas and, with a slight tremble in his hand, turned on the radio. Opera blared from the speakers.

"Turn that shit off," ordered the baby from the back seat.

With a sigh, the brute obeyed. Then he started drumming on the steering wheel with his thick thumbs.

"Sweet Baby Geezie, Ram, why are you so nervous? It's not like you."

"The Gelatin District always gives me the jitters."

"Well, your nervousness is making me nervous, so stop it."

Violet Greene lived on Pig Innards Place—a road that was actually paved with bone chips from a slaughterhouse—in a squat brick apartment building called the Gristle Arms. It was one of the nicer places in the Gelatin District, as a majority of the windows were still intact and there were no dead bodies living on the stoop.

Ram parked near a rusted fire hydrant and carried the baby toward the building, keeping a wary eye on the many shadows that blanketed the Gelatin District, even in the middle of the day.

Jaydon spotted a ripped Senator Dove poster plastered to the side of the Gristle Arms. The poster was so defaced the baby could barely make out the nutless politician. Thinking that the political poster had probably been put up by Ruby Redd gave Jaydon a weird feeling in his stomach. Or maybe it was just gas.

At the front door, they encountered locks that were locked with locks, an alarm of alarming size, and an intercom that, surprisingly, worked. Ram gaped at the device as if it had been fashioned from the Swedish language.

"Go 'head," ordered Jaydon, "ring Violet's apartment. Standing out here in the open makes my flesh crawl, and I know a lot about crawling."

Looking deep into his boss's baby blues, Ram said, "You know, boss, sometimes the past is like a rock and it's best not to turn it over. You might not like what you find underneath."

"Thanks for the advice, Hallmark. Perhaps it's what I'll carve into your gravestone when I kill you for not ringing that fucking bell!"

Nodding imperceptibly, Ram buzzed Violet's apartment. Nothing happened for a few moments.

"Well, she ain't here," concluded Ram, ready to turn and run. "Let's you and me go get a drink in a nice part of town, maybe talk about our gangsterless future."

"Patience, Ram, patience," the baby said impatiently.

Finally, the intercom sprang to life. Violet's voice came through tinny but true. "If this is Mr. Havensack again, the answer is still no, I'm not gonna fuck you. I don't care how many chocolate bars you claim to have hidden in your bunker."

Jaydon piped up, communicating the sneer on his face through the sound of his voice. "I don't care to fuck you, Violet, but thanks for the kind offer. This is Kid Phoenix."

"But you're... you're..."

"Yeah, yeah, I'm dead, now tell me something I don't know."

"Sweet Baby Geezie, please tell me you haven't come back as a zombie. I hate them things."

"Give me a little credit, Violet. People are so tired of zombies. I'm a cute little baby. I've been reincarnated and shit. So just let me in and I'll fill you in on the particulars."

"If you're looking for Ruby Redd, Kid, she ain't here and I honestly don't know where she is."

He could hear fear in her voice and it felt good to him, like he was drinking a warm bottle. He said, "Listen, my name is Jaydon now and, regardless of how fucking gay it sounds, that's what I want to be called."

"I'm sorry. I'm sorry... Jaydon. Maybe... maybe you should talk to Paulo down at Stripping Through History. He might know something about something."

"I would, but he's kind of dead now. Listen, Violet. Me and my cute little dimples are a little worried standing out here in your shitty neighborhood. I just heard on the radio that another rabid ocelot has escaped from the zoo, and you know how those things can rip your face off before you can scream. So let me the fuck in."

Uneasy, Ram shifted from foot to foot.

Through the intercom, Violet said, "I don't... I don't know if that's a good idea."

"No, you know what a bad idea is, Violet? Pissing me off right now is a bad idea. I'm already edgy. I haven't had my morning nap and that fucking ocelot is running around with faces in his fucking mouth. Continue to piss me off and I'll have Ram here—you remember Ram Bountybar, big, dumb, mean—I'll have Ram here rip this fucking door out by its roots. Then our discussion won't be so pleasant. It won't be about figuring out which frumpy Bella Abzug outfit to wear. It will be about me having this brute kick the shit out of you while you answer my questions. An experience, I might add, that not many people have lived through."

There was a loud buzz and the door swung wide and slow like a prison door.

The elevator in the Gristle Arms had been stolen ages ago so Ram and Jaydon had to take the stairs. Well, it was technically just Ram who slowly ascended the stairs since Jaydon was resting in the large man's arms. Not that he was restful—he was squirming, his face flushed.

"Geez, Ram, do you always got to move so slow? We got business here."

Ram picked up the pace a bit. Found the binky in his pocket, blew off some of the lint, and shoved it into the baby's mouth to get him to stop the complaining.

At the end of their three-flight journey, they found Violet's door as open as a whore's legs. She was waiting for them, standing in the middle of her living room. Staring at the threadbare floor and dressed in a pink robe that had seen better days, her shoulders slumped with defeat dragging down the corners of her mouth, which was caked with her distinctive green lipstick.

"I don't wanna die, Kid," she said without looking up. "I ain't done nothing wrong." Pulling out his binky, Jaydon asked, "Who says you're gonna die, gorgeous?"

When Violet finally did raise her head, shock played across her face. "Sweet Baby Geezie, Kid, I thought you was joking. You really are a kid."

"That's true, but still as dangerous as diaper rash. And I want to be called by my birth name, Jaydon. It's really starting to grow on me."

The shaken woman shook again and said, "Sorry, I forgot. So you wanna sit? You want something to drink? I mean, do you even... do you even drink now that you're like... that?"

"What I want is answers. Before Ram here stomped the poor fuck to death, Paulo reminded me that Ruby Redd quit the stripping biz, wanted to start a family."

"Yeah, she, uh, she'd mentioned she wanted to, you know, procreate and such."

"Just not with me."

Locking her eyes on the baby, Violet said, "She thought—and these are her words, not mine—but she thought that you weren't mature enough to raise kids."

"Not mature enough?!?" squealed Jaydon, fussing, kicking, turning red. "Who was it, Violet? Who was fucking my gal?"

Something broke in Violet Greene. She fell to her chubby knees as if preparing to shoot craps. Tears rushed forth and she babbled nonsense.

"Sweet Baby Geezie, Ram, give her this to calm her down." Jaydon held out his binky. The henchman hesitated, not knowing whether his boss was serious or not. But Jaydon jabbed him with the binky repeatedly.

Taking the pacifier, Ram jammed it in the babbling stripper's mouth. For a moment, she sucked on it, which really did calm her down.

Spitting the pinky out on the carpet, she screamed, "You can't win her back, Kid! She's married! And she finally found someone who everyone loves. He's a million times better than you, a million times more powerful! A guy you can't possibly touch!"

Jaydon felt his baby blood pressure rise. "Married?!? More powerful than me?!? Where is she? Tell me!"

"I ain't never gonna tell you!"

"Punch her, Ram! Punch her right in the fucking areola!"

"I don't, I don't think I can."

"Then punch her anywhere on her tit!"

"I mean, I can't hit her anywhere, boss. She's a woman. I don't hit women."

The gangster baby squirmed so much that Ram nearly dropped him. "I've had about enough of your guff, Ram. Geezie, when did you lose your balls?"

But before the brute could divulge the whereabouts of his testes, the grimy window behind Violet shattered. Glass clattered, and in leapt a large ocelot, all stripped and spotted and rabid. Licking its lips.

Ram screamed, "I thought you made up the escaped ocelot!"

"So did I!"

Hungry for face, the ocelot growled and launched himself at Violet, who was closest to him. As she went down beneath the beautiful pelt, Violet screamed, "You'll never find her, Kid, never! And Jaydon is far and away the gayest name in Marrowburg!"

After the first bite, Ram scuttered toward the door.

"Get my binky, dickhead, get my binky!"

Careful not to interrupt the ocelot's lunch, Ram lunged forward. Grabbing the pacifier, which was now smeared with green lipstick, Ram spun, fled. Taking the stairs three at a time, he was certain he'd never get the sound of Violet getting eaten out of his mind.

Chapter Ten

The Bamboo Diaphragm of Love

When the patrol cart rolled to a stop outside of Striping Through History, Bertrand turned to his new partner and said, "You're going to have to carry me, rook."

"What?"

"To the crime scene, you're going to have to carry me. Sometimes my legs don't work so well. Probably because they've been kicking criminal ass for over eighty years!"

Officer-For-A-Day Thimbleton stared at the old man, shook his head slowly. "That's crazy."

Groaning, Bertrand reached out with a hand turned purple from liver spots and very deliberately grabbed Thimbleton by the collar. Tried to pull him close, but didn't have the strength. "Listen, rook, I know we don't get along, and we never will, but we're partners now and we have to work together."

"But Dream Comers never said–"

"Oh, fuck those lefties down at Dream Comers. Listen kid, let me let you in on something. Life deals you a hand and you got to play that hand. Your hand is that you got to carry me to the crime scene. But first, we have to stop off at the bathroom for a pee. Be warned, you'll have to hold my penis as my grip isn't so good and I don't want to piss on my shoes. They're only twenty years old."

It took them several minutes to get to the crime scene since Bertrand's bladder refused to cooperate for quite some time and, after the urination episode, Thimbleton spent a long time at the sink, washing his hands repeatedly and whimpering.

In Paulo's office, where the club owner was murdered, Bertrand sat on the leopard skin couch and took his noon meds, dozens of pills of various shapes and sizes, which

48

supposedly assuaged everything from his thin blood to his failing memory. Thimbleton studied Paulo, his body sprawled, his eyes wide, his mouth hanging.

"What's the matter, kid? Ain't never seen a dead body before?"

Thimbleton, unable to find the words, shook his head.

Bertrand would have laughed had he been certain that his dentures would have stayed in. "Well, you better get used to it. You'll be dead soon yourself. Say, what's in the poor fucker's mouth anyway?"

"It looks... it looks like a baby's rattle."

"Well, kid, pull it out. It's obviously what killed him. Therefore, it's evidence."

His hands shaking, Officer-For-A-Day Thimbleton reached for the rattle, trying desperately not to touch the dead man's dead skin. Pulling the rattle free, the dying kid groaned and held it high for Bertrand to see.

"Cripes," said Bertrand, "now I have really seen everything. Alright, put that in one of our evidence burlap sacks and bring me someone to interview."

The first interviewee was a stripper who made Bertrand's heart hurt. Or maybe he was just having another stroke.

This full figured woman wore a drab dress, long and gray, and a matching hat. But she moved with confidence. Strode into the room and took a seat across from Bertrand, who stared at her as if she were a ghost.

Thimbleton said, "Admittedly, ma'am, I don't have a lot of experience with the strippers, but aren't you supposed to wear things that show off your naughty parts?"

The woman fixed him with a bemused stare. "Here at Stripping Through History, we believe that men can learn as they are getting their rocks off. All of us gals studied History or Women's Studies at Marrowburg Community College and Dry Cleaning Service and now we try to spread the gospel of equality while taking off our clothes."

Thimbleton, who was too busy dying to take classes, asked, "So, who are you supposed to be then? Jackie Kennedy?"

"No, you boob, she's obviously Margaret Sanger, an early feminist who was elemental in establishing birth control in this country."

The young woman smiled at the old man appreciatively. "You have a good memory for history."

"Something like that," said the old man, drifting back into his memories.

It was the summer of 1931. The air hung heavy with humidity and smelled of skillet-fried excrement. Officer Kropp, on his first beat, was walking the cracked sidewalks of Marrowburg, attempting to keep the peace while sweating to death. Via carrier pigeon, the young cop had gotten called to the scene of a birth control rally in Pickled Pig's Feet Park. A middle-aged woman, Margaret Sanger, was giving an impassioned speech to a crowd of females who, despite the heat, were energetically clapping and cheering. It was hard to know whether the women were excited over the feminist's fervent speech or anxious to see a little blood spilled in the Marrowburg tradition of assassinating anyone famous who happened into town.

Besides the females assembled, many priests from St. Jude's Catholic Church and Off-Track Betting were loitering, protesting the protest. With their hatchet faces and fisty hands, the men of God were spoiling for a fight. Though he was new to the force, Officer Kropp knew he was about to have a riot on his hands.

Pushing his way through the crowd, Bertrand had to take action, but when he saw Margaret Sanger's face, everything stopped. A bout of second sight hit him right where it hurt: his heart. In his swirling head, he saw himself and Margaret Sanger riding away from a church atop a patrol cart affixed with a sign that read: JUST MARRIED. They kissed passionately as rice rained down.

He snapped out of his reverie when he got hit in back of his head with a stale Eucharist host hurled by one of the angry priests.

Hoping to prevent any bloodshed, the young cop jumped onstage and arrested Margaret Sanger. He was roundly booed by both the women and the priests.

"On what grounds are you arresting me?" demanded Sanger, her eyes flashing like brown lightning.

"Failure to..." and he mumbled something that he hoped sounded technical and police-y, praying she wouldn't notice he was faking his way through this arrest.

"What did you say?"

Pulling her close, he whispered in her ear, "Listen, I'm just trying to save your sweet ass. These priests are out for blood."

She scoffed. "I've dealt with priests before."

"Not like these priests, lady. They're Marrowburg priests. There's nothing that brings them closer to the Sweet Baby Geezie than doling out a little punishment. I once saw them crucify a boy just because he forgot to thank them for his morning beating."

Although he was done discussing the matter, Sanger fought him as he pulled her from the stage. He couldn't help but notice that, during their tussle, her dress tore, exposing her left breast and its corresponding nipple. The cop tried not to stare, but the whole set-up was pretty sweet. Especially for a forty-year-old woman who had probably spat out a couple of kids.

Kropp dragged the feminist and her exposed breast through the crowd of women, who belted him with moldy potatoes and recently used oaken diaphragms.

The cop and his collar never would have made it out of that lady crowd alive if it hadn't been for the priests and their bloodlust. They clashed with the women, cracking skulls with large crucifixes and laughing manically. While the melee swelled around him, Bertrand realized that he'd started the riot he so hoped to avoid. Cursing himself, the young cop snuck out with Sanger and disappeared into the sweltering streets of Marrowburg.

"Where are you taking me?" she demanded when they were clear of the crowd.

"To the nearest station house to book you."

And then, someday, you'll forgive me and marry me and we'll live happily ever after, thought the young policeman.

"Listen, I can't spend the night in jail. My two sons are back at the hotel."

"Well, you should have thought of that before you incited that riot."

Sanger dug in her heels and their progress stopped. "I wasn't inciting anything, I was simply talking about birth control."

Attempting to hide the fact that he was staring at her open-air boob, Bertrand minted the term, "Tough titty."

"Hey, listen, maybe we can work out a deal...."

"Are you trying to bribe me?"

"You look like the type of guy who hasn't had a lot of women."

Kropp snorted. He'd had exactly zero women. "I get my fair share."

"Okay, great, killer. What if you and I just ducked into one of these alleys and had a little fun and then you let me go?"

"By 'fun,' you mean something of a sexual nature, right? I'm terrible at board games."

Confused, Sanger nodded.

The young cop considered his situation. If he did take her to a station house, he'd have to explain why he arrested her and he didn't really have a good reason. Besides, the last time he'd been within striking distance of a woman's dirty parts was when he was born.

"Okay," said Bertrand, "but on one condition."

"Name it."

"You can't laugh at me."

Trying to keep a straight face, Sanger promised.

Hand in hand, they ducked into the alley. When she pulled out her bamboo diaphragm, which was beautifully embroidered with her initials (MS), he asked if they were going to have soup first. This excited him, as he really enjoyed a good bowl of soup.

Biting her lip to keep from laughing, she explained that this was the newest in wooden contraception from Japan. Much more flexible than the old oaken diaphragms women were using.

He asked where they would brew the soup.

Using small words, she attempted to explain what a diaphragm was. About four words into her explanation, Bertrand blanched and achieved orgasm right in his gabardines. He didn't know if this was brought on by Sanger's use of the term "woman's pee-pee area" or simply the promise of soup. The stain across his pants was sticky and looked like a question mark.

Laughing so hard she dropped the bamboo diaphragm, Sanger pushed past him. "Well, thanks for showing a lady a good time," she called over her feminist shoulder.

She disappeared out of the mouth of the alley and out of his life, the woman he almost technically lost his virginity to. The woman he dreamed of marrying.

Shaking his head to clear the historical cobwebs, Bertrand found himself back in Paulo's office with Thimbleton and the stripper staring at him.

"Mr. Kropp, are you okay? Should I get you a glass of water or something?" asked Thimbleton.

Wiping away some tiny tears with shaking hands, Bertrand assured everyone that he was okay. "I was just thinking about the case. So, Ms. Sanger, did you see anyone unusual in the club today?"

"Everyone in this club is unusual."

Bertrand nodded then nodded off. That happened a lot these days—slipping into sleep right in the middle of a conversation.

The faux Margaret Sanger looked at the faux cop and asked, "Is he dead?"

"Gee, I hope not," replied Thimbleton, not sure if he actually felt that way or not.

"Well, whether he's dead or sleeping, you wanna learn something new?" said the stripper. "I've always been turned on by older guys."

Thimbleton didn't have the nerve to tell her the truth.

Swiveling toward the officer-for-a-day, she spread her legs. He could see all the way up to her pee-pee area. Being a virgin, this was new territory to him. Though trembling, he moved closer to her, placed a wrinkly hand on her leg. He knew this was wrong on so many levels, but his life was running out and he didn't want to die a virgin. He wanted to go out with a bang.

Closing her eyes, the stripper moaned, "Margaret Sanger, née Higgins, was born on September 14th, 1879 in New York City. Her parents were Michael Hennessey Higgins, a stonemason and freethinker, and Anne Purcell Higgins..."

Chapter Eleven

The Local FBOA Meeting

Sucking on a lollipop, Baby Jaydon cackled and said, "Just like taking candy from a baby." Narrowing his eyes, the baby glared at Ram in the rearview mirror. "Not that I'm trying to give you any smart ideas."

What the tiny gangster was referring to was the ease with which they had found Rinky Dink. It was as simple as checking out the local Face Burned Off Anonymous meetings. This particular FBOA meeting was being held in the basement of the St. Jude Catholic Church and Off-Track Betting. While Jaydon napped, dreaming of giraffes going round and round, Ram had snuck up and looked through the window, finding their quarry amongst the other horribly disfigured people sitting in a circle of folding chairs, drinking coffee, and pouring out their souls.

Jaydon's crack about stealing his candy didn't get a response from Ram, who was looking out the window, distracted. The baby gangster asked, "What's up your ass, Ram?"

"I dunno. I mean, what are we doing? Maybe we should just leave everything alone. Ruby Redd is married and, well, maybe she's happy."

"The fuck she married twisted me."

"Well, yeah, but..." Ram didn't finish his thought and Jaydon didn't care.

They sat in silence until the meeting ended and the disfigured emerged into the sunshine. There was about twelve of them, smoking cigarettes, which seemed like a bad idea.

Standing in their midst was a nun. Dropping his sucker, Jaydon studied her. As his skin boiled, everything inside of him froze.

Her drab black habit could not hide the woman's delicious curves. Jayden swore he spotted a lick of red hair sticking out of her wimple.

It can't be... there's no way in hell....

Closing his eyes, Jaydon shook his bulbous head and convinced himself that what he'd seen was nothing but a dream, a mirage, a vision. Then he looked back at disbanding FBOA meeting, but the nun was gone. Having Ruby Redd on his brain had forced him into seeing things, crazy things.

He got back to the business at hand.

The scarred were disbanding, heading separate directions.

"Follow the burned fucker," ordered Jaydon. "Close but don't give us away. Let's see where he's going."

After biding a farewell to his scorched friends, Rinky headed down the street, walking like a man who had no particular place to go.

This went on for several blocks. The baby grew impatient, started fussing. "At the next alley, let's grab him. Have a little discussion."

Sighing loudly, Ram pulled into the alley, jumped from the vehicle.

"Don't forget me," wailed the baby, kicking his tiny pink feet.

Freeing the infant from his constraints, Ram cradled him and spun to confront Rinky Dink. Rinky knitted his brow, studied the brute with the baby in his arms, said, "Hey, Ram. Cute kid."

"I'm not cute," spat Jaydon. "I'm your fucking worst nightmare."

Rinky drew back. "Sweet Baby Geezie, Ram. You should really get your kid to watch his mouth."

"I ain't his kid, Rinky. I'm his fucking boss."

Narrowing his eyes, Rinky Dink said, "Hey, I know that voice."

"Of course you do, you asshole."

Looking as if he was having a coronary, the burned man grabbed his chest. "Is that you, Kid?"

Jaydon smiled and colorful sucker juice sluiced down his chin. "Now which one of us is shitting our pants?"

"Kid," said Rinky, his voice ragged, "if you're looking for Ruby Redd, she's... she's already moved on."

"Tell me something I don't know, Rinky. She got a new guy so she could have a kid."

Rinky laughed a nervous a little laugh. "The guy she's married to can't have kids, you uninformed little–"

Moving surprisingly fast, Ram grabbed Rinky by the collar. Pulled him deep into the coolness and the darkness of the alley, the smell of garbage and urine mixing with his natural French onion bouquet. Hard, Ram shoved him against the brick wall. Some flies flew.

Burned lips barely formed the words "But, Ram, you... you–"

"Shut up, Rinky," said Jaydon, "I'm doing the squawking here. Right before I had Ram rattle the life out of him, Paulo said that you was the one who delivered the message to me about meeting someone in the alley that night some fuck twisted me. So who gave you that note?"

His eyes, like two blazing guns, looked back and forth between the baby and Ram. He tried to speak, but nothing came.

With his free hand, Ram punched Rinky right in his scarred nose. There was a sound, like lightning hitting a TNT warehouse, and Rinky went down, breaking gravity's speed limit.

Twisting spastically, his limbs waving uncontrollably, Jaydon turned on Ram. "What ya do that for?"

"He wasn't talking. It was making me crazy. Don't worry, I'll get him to spill the beans. As a baby, you shouldn't have to see this."

Gently, the giant put the infant down, leaned him against a mound of moldy garbage bags facing away from the action.

"I wanna see. I wanna see, you stupid thug!"

"Sorry, boss, I don't wanna emotionally scar you."

Over his own bawling, Jaydon heard Ram beat the other man savagely. He heard bones and brick breaking, blood being spilt. He pictured shattered teeth and bruised flesh, and a bubbly smile formed on his lips.

Then the beating stopped. The air was quiet except for flies.

Huffing and puffing, Ram said, "Whadya say, Rinky? What?"

With his tiny balled fists, Jaydon grabbed the garbage bag he was leaning against and pulled with all his might. Falling over onto the grimy pavement, he landed on a disintegrating bamboo diaphragm that had MS embroidered on it. Disgusting, but at least now he had a good view of the action. Ram was kneeling next to the battered and bloodied Rinky, his ear to the man's mouth, which was moving soundlessly.

Shaking his head, Ram stood, cleaned his hands off in an oily puddle. He looked as if he were the one who'd taken the beating.

"What did he say?" the gangster baby inquired.

His head hanging, the large man made his way back to the baby, picked him up. "He said it was Semple Skehill who gave him that note."

Jaydon registered his surprise by spitting up all the lollipop juice in his system. It coated Ram's shoulder with crimson. "But that don't make no sense, Semple Skehill is just a worthless drunk."

"Boss, he swore to it with his dying breath. I think we gotta assume he wasn't lying."

Chapter Twelve

Fucking Faux Margaret Sanger

Bertrand awoke with a start. The old cop was disheartened to find a naked Thimbleton pressed into an equally naked and faux Margaret Sanger on the floor—extremely close to the dead body of Paulo Banko—their tongues twinning, glistening. With one final thrust, the officer-for-a-day cried out, slumped, and lay against the stripper, spent. She ran a sweaty hand through his sweaty hair, said, "... and Ms. Sanger died of congestive heart failure in Tucson, Arizona at the age of eight-six. There, now you know everything."

With a touch of anger, Bertrand cleared his throat.

The couple broke apart and Thimbleton stared at him. "Oh, sorry, Mr. Kropp. We thought you were dead."

"No, I'm the opposite of dead. I was experiencing my second sight. I saw a man, a man on a horse. There were flames burning brightly behind him. He shot an arrow into poor Paulo's chest."

Officer-For-A-Day Thimbleton alternated between dressing his saggy ancient body and staring at Bertrand as if he'd lost his marbles.

The old cop was familiar with this reaction. His life was a long series of people staring at him with their mouths hanging open and shaking their heads.

When he was still in diapers, his grandmother—who considered herself something of a witch—laid her gnarled hands upon his befuddled head and declared that he'd been blessed with "the Gift" as he had been having some pretty weird dreams. She asserted that Bertrand could see things that other people couldn't, things that weren't necessarily there. At least that's what the old woman thought, but she

59

also fervently believed that cardboard came from cows and that Grover Cleveland was sending her messages from beyond the grave through her toilet plunger.

After his grandmother passed, there weren't a lot of people left who believed in Bertrand's visions. Certainly, there was the rare occasion when he could lead a child to a missing glove or find where his mother had hidden his lunch, but, much more often, his intuitions led to people wandering around a vacant lot all night looking for a lost cat and finding only cans. His sad success rate did little to curb his visions. He was constantly consulting neighbors about where they could find their missing possessions, even if said possessions weren't even missing.

One thing that Bertrand never found was a friend. Around the neighborhood, he was thought of as a freak.

It was his unusual—and possibly imagined—"Gift" that led the young Kropp to the local station house. When he was a lad of sixteen, one of the young women on his block, Sally Mendzela, disappeared. During a nap, it was revealed to Bertrand that the missing girl was at the bottom of the Rendering River, stuck in the branches of an underwater tree, blue and bloated. This revelation was understandably upsetting to the mother of the poor girl, who insisted that it couldn't be true. At least the bloated part, as little Sally had only been gone for a few hours. Undeterred, Bertrand marched down to the station house with his information.

The cops, bored, acted on his tip by dragging the Rendering River for the missing girl's body. They didn't find a bloated and blue Sally Mendzela—she turned up, unharmed, a few hours later (she hadn't been missing so much as hanging out in the local library)—but they did find something much more valuable (and much less gross): an all mahogany, pearl-inlaid croquette set. Marrowburg cops, when not taking bribes, loved playing a little full-contact croquette. In celebration, the cops (who were quite drunk) rewarded Bertrand and his second sight with the job of Officer Third Class on the force.

And now, eighty-four years later, when he told Thimbleton his theories concerning the man on horseback, the Officer-For-A-Day could only shake his head.

The faux cop sputtered, "Wait, Mr. Kropp, don't you think one of the, ah, well, strippers would have noticed a man with a horse ride into the club?"

"And," pointed out the faux Margaret Sanger, "Paulo was choked to death, not shot with an arrow."

"Oh," said Bertrand. "Right. Well, it's time for my next round of meds and they have to be taken with food, so let's grab some lunch."

Chapter Thirteen

Death Comes to Pervy Claus

It was roundly agreed among the ne'er-do-wells of Marrowburg that Club Club was the most dangerous (and therefore enjoyable) drinking establishment in the city. Located in an abandoned slaughterhouse on the East Side, Club Club had a higher murder rate than most American cities. That's possibly because everyone who entered Club Club was handed a large wooden club that was to be used to settle any disagreements that occurred whilst drinking. These clubs were used to settle every argument from men coming onto a claimed woman to color preferences.

Club Club was made for men like Semple Skehill, a lush who'd forgotten his own real name, and Ram thought it was the perfect place to start looking for the drunk.

When the brute entered Club Club with Jaydon napping in a Baby Bjorn—another baby-related "gift" left by his sister in her car—strapped to his massive chest, he got the once over twice from the mug handing out the clubs. "There's a drinking age, you know."

"I'm aware, he don't drink."

"And we ain't got any clubs that will fit in his tiny hands."

"That's fine, we ain't here to fight. We're just looking for somebody."

"Alright, but if that baby gets clubbed, know that his blood is not on my hands."

"Noted."

Side-stepping a large puddle of congealed ejaculate, Ram waded into the club and the noise of the jukebox brought Kid back to the land of the awake. "Where the fuck... oh, Club Club. Good call, Ram."

The henchman replied with a quick nod and began trolling the copious shadows of the club, staring into every booth. Thugs and molls by the boatload, but no Semple Skehill.

"He ain't here, boss," surmised Ram.

"I can see that, dumbass, I got eyes. Let's have a word with the barkeep. Maybe he can point us in the right direction."

At the bar, the bartender was half-heartedly breaking up an argument between a shoe salesman and a parrot.

Ram waved for his attention. "I got a question."

"I hope it ain't geography," said the barkeep.

"Sort of. We're wondering where Semple Skehill is located."

"That's an easy one. Evergreen Cemetery, six feet beneath the surface of the earth. His liver finally imploded."

Jaydon spit up a little in surprise.

"Well, boss, it looks like the guy who killed you got his already," chirped Ram, wiping the puddle of sick from Jaydon's chin.

"I wanted to kill the fuck!" shouted the baby, struggling to kick his way out of the Baby Bjorn.

To calm his boss, Ram stuck the pacifier in his mouth.

Behind them, a voice thundered out, shaking the dingy bar to its very knees. A feminine voice, crackling with death and dangerousness, said, "Hey, you son-of-a-bitch, turn around so I can watch you watch me kill you."

Since there wasn't a man present who didn't assume his life couldn't be snuffed short by some irate female at any given time, every single person at the bar affixed a phony smile, gently set their clubs down next to their drinks, and turned to face their possible demises.

Standing in the middle of the bar was a woman who was so short she was borderline midget. The fashion in which she was dressed betrayed the fact that she'd never set a single high heel in such a lowly establishment. She looked like a cupcake with legs: rounded, pink, and fluffy. Her hair—and there was a disturbing amount of the stuff—was dyed the same hue of pink as her outfit and piled high, nearly brushing the cigarette-stained ceiling. She wore about four pounds of make-up, all of it some shade of pink. In one gloved hand she clutched a well-groomed dog, in the other: a well-groomed gun.

Which seemed to be aimed straight at Jaydon's head, a situation that he didn't particularly care for. On the verge of a meltdown, he had to admit to himself that he wanted his Mommy. Too bad he killed her.

Taking the binky out of his mouth, Jaydon said, "Listen, lady, I don't know–"

"Shut up, pipsqueak." Both her voice and her eyes were steel. "Surely you remember me. I'm Bonnie Voyage, owner of Good Travel, the number one travel agency in all of Marrowburg. Or, I should say, for the record and for the police report, the *former* number one travel agency in all of Marrowburg. In the last nine months, my business and my life have gone to hell, and it's all because of you."

The baby studied the crazy lady. Although he'd been in a serious relationship with Ruby Redd, there had been other women, a little strange on the side to pass the time, but this irate quasi-midget certainly didn't ring any bells. Jaydon said, "I'm sorry, but I have no idea–"

"I'm the one doing the talking here! Former award-winning travel agents have the floor now! Everyone in this godforsaken bar is going to listen to my sad story of ruination!" A tear—Jaydon swore it was pink—slid down her powdery face and jumped to its death on the filthy floor. The joint was so quiet that everyone heard the pathetic PLOP!

"Nine months ago, you wandered into Good Travel travel agency, begging me for a five-star vacation package. It had to have all the bells and whistles: sandy beaches, ocean front grass huts, banana daiquiris. And you wanted it to start that very night with first class tickets on a midnight plane. It was an impossible request, but I took it for two reasons: I love a good challenge and I could tell that you were really in love by the way you spoke about your lady friend. So I called in every favor I was owed and made ridiculous promises, most of them sexual, that I knew I couldn't keep, all because I love love. With all my hard work and my vaginal promises, I made your dream happen. But when you didn't show up that night, and I couldn't find you, I lost my shirt. Since then, it's been nine months of bad luck, which ended today when I happened to see you walking down the street and followed you into this hellhole, where I plan to end your life."

"Lady," piped up Jaydon, "there's something screwy going on here. I think you got the wrong baby. I ain't never clapped eyes on your pinkness before. And by "pinkness," I don't mean your snatch, though I love a good snatch, as one can tell by my tattoo, and I'm sure yours is nice and pink and–"

"I'm not talking to–"

"Look out, boss, she's gonna shoot!" exclaimed Ram.

And so she did. But not before Ram, with his free hand, grabbed the unlucky son-of-a-bitch who happened to be planted beside him and tossed him straight into the line of fire. He barely had time to curse the Sweet Baby Geezie before a bullet tore through his throat.

Dead and gone, the unlucky son-of-a-bitch folded to the floor with a dearth of drama.

The swift movement had torn the straps on the Baby Bjorn. Jaydon, falling to the floor and screaming his tiny head off about it, was grabbed by Ram not two inches from the floor.

All hell, which was always close at hand at Club Club, broke loose. Everyone grabbed their provided clubs and began swinging wildly. Skulls got cracked, noses got broken, and, worst of all, whiskeys were spilt.

Tucking the baby under his arm like a football, Ram returned to his glorious gridiron days by taking off for the goal line, which, in this case, was an overturned table near the entrance.

Shocked, Jaydon spat his pacifier out on the floor and forgot about it.

"No one screws with Bonnie Voyage and lives to brag about it," the pink human vowed and, dropping the poodle like a hot potato, squeezed off another round at the fleeing and former football player. It whizzed past Jaydon's soft fontanel like a mosquito with blood on its mind.

"That's easily the craziest travel agent I've ever dealt with," Jaydon screamed over the tumult.

Still running, Ram agreed. "She is saying some really crazy shit. Hold on."

Aiming for the safety of the overturned table, Ram leapt. Despite the brute's best attempts to tuck and roll, the pair landed badly behind the table. Ram cried out in pain, felt something in his shoulder go all funny.

Jaydon and Ram quickly discovered they weren't alone in their hiding place. It was already occupied by an old man with a matted white beard and a stained red suit.

"Hey, Pervy Claus," said Jaydon. Everyone knew this distinctive Marrowburg ne'er-do-well.

"Hey, baby, what do you want for Christmas?"

"This shooting to stop."

"Why? This is the best dust-up Club Club has hosted in many a moon," said the old man, unmistakably giddy. He laughed and his belly shook like a bowl full of past-date jelly.

Though the bar brawl was deafening—people clubbing the hell out of their fellow man, chairs smashing, the pained screams of the injured—Jaydon could clearly hear the *clickclickclick* of high heels getting closer and closer. This sound scared him down to his still-fusing bones.

Shaking his arms and legs uncontrollably, the baby barked, "Quick, Ram, pull out your piece!"

His head hanging, the lackey admitted that he'd left his .44 in the car. Jaydon muttered something derisive about the henchman's mental abilities.

Rising arthritically, Pervy Claus got to his pegs. "This has been fun, but I must be moving along. It's Condom Night at the Marrowburg Retirement Village and Ice Hockey Training Center."

With great difficulty, the old man attempted to shuffle toward the door. He and his beard made it about eight inches before one of the travel agent's bullets found him and made a home in his back. The old man fell to the floor, blood leaving his body like rats leaving a sinking ship.

After birthing a substantial horsy in his diaper, Jaydon shouted, "We gotta get outta here before that bitch perforates us."

"Too late," hissed Bonnie Voyage.

The brute and the baby turned to find the armed woman towering over them. The gun made her look taller, less cupcake-y. She held the weapon steady with both deadly hands; the poodle apparently haven taken a powder. She said, "In case you're wondering, I got you the Bridal Yurt at the fabulous Trump Leper Colony and Casinos on St. Barts. Six days, seven nights, right on the fucking beach!"

Smiling as if she'd sent all her marbles on a long vacation, the travel agent leveled the gun right at the baby.

"Do not fuck with me right now, bitch, I'm teething!" With all his baby might, Jaydon leapt from Ram's chest and landed on the floor near the lady's high heels. Before she could even react, he clamped his two new teeth squarely onto her pink ankle. Biting down, he felt his mouth fill with blood, tangy yet sweet. It was like mother's milk to the gangster baby.

Bonnie Voyage screamed with vigor and her next shot went wildly astray, killing a light that hung above them. Glass sleeted down.

The frantic travel agent shook her leg as if performing a new dance craze sweeping the nation, but Jaydon held on tight. He knew that if he let go, he'd be taking up residence next to Semple Skehill in the Evergreen Cemetery.

"This is exactly why I didn't have children!" cried Bonnie Voyage, tears of rage pelting the floor.

That was the last bitchy thing that bitch ever bitched about in her bitch-filled life. For while Jaydon and Bonnie Voyage were battling, Ram rose to his feet. Balling his massive fist, he socked the travel agent square in the jaw. Jaydon felt the reverberation of this punch clear down in her ankle. Her head now at a very uncomfortable-looking angle, she dropped the gun and crumpled into a pile of pink.

With a twinge of regret, Jaydon unhinged his jaw and let go of Bonnie Voyage's ankle. Marveled at the nice ring of teeth marks.

Man, Jaydon thought, *my fucking baby teeth are really coming in nicely!*

Before the travel agent even had time to move or bitch, Ram was upon her, straddling her. This would have appeared sexual if Ram's eyes weren't brimming with calm rage.

Growling lightly, Ram grabbed Bonnie Voyage's head and smashed it against the floor. Just once. Like a ripe melon, her cranium split in two and blood and brains seeped out, staining her pink red.

Not that the death of the travel agent had any effect on the bar brawl, which continued, unabated.

Hands slick with travel agent blood, Ram picked up the baby and scrambled toward the door, avoiding swung chairs and swung fists.

Somewhere behind them, a dog was yap, yap, yapping.

Chapter Fourteen

Big Black's Hut of Steaming Entrails

Riding high on a post-virginity buzz and bursting with feminist knowledge, Thimbleton sat atop the police cart in the parking lot of Big Black's Hut of Steaming Entrails, eating a foot-long Marrowburg Steamer—a foot-long hotdog smothered with chocolate pudding—and preaching Margaret Sanger.

"... and on October 16th, 1916, Margaret Sanger opened a birth control clinic in Brooklyn, the first of its kind in the nation."

Bertrand, picturing the real Margaret Sanger and his proto-sex act with her, grumbled and made a loose swipe at one of the many flies that called Big Black's Hut of Steaming Entrails home.

He had much to grumble about.

Afraid the old man would choke, Thimbleton wouldn't allow the old man his own hot dog from Big Black's Hut of Steaming Entrails. Sitting beside Thimbleton, Bertrand was stuck sucking on ketchup packets, not saying a word but registering complaint with his every suck.

Not that the officer-for-a-day, so recently having gotten his rocks off, noticed.

Relishing his new life as a real man, Thimbleton took a giant bite of his Marrowburg Steamer. His mouth clogged with entrails and chocolate pudding, the faux cop rhapsodized, "Sweet Baby Geezie, that's good. You know, the Marrowburg Steamer is to hot dogs what Margaret Sanger is to feminists."

While most hot dogs in the world tried to hide their dark origins, Big Black did not believe in such subterfuge. At his restaurant (Big Black's Hut of Steaming Entrails was really just a condemned shack within choking distance of the Rendering River), his dogs were fashioned from entrails and the public was well aware of this fact. Not that such information kept Marrowburgites away; they flocked to Big Black's like pigs to a trough. Especially on Thursday when it was All-You-Can-Stomach Tuesdays.

Just as Thimbleton was about to launch into a quasi-fascinating tale about how Margaret Sanger started *The Birth Control Review*, which had been told to him by the randy yet knowledgeable stripper, a carrier pigeon fluttered onto Bertrand's head and crapped copiously, ruining the dying kid's meal and his story. Though it took him a few flailing attempts, Bertrand captured the bird and slowly read the message carved into its belly, his lips moving as he read. When he finished, he glared at the ground.

Since patience isn't something most Progeria Syndrome patients are known for, Thimbleton demanded to know what the carrier pigeon had told Bertrand.

Following standard police procedure, the old man tried to wring the carrier pigeon's neck—Captain Milktwat always feared police messages would fall into enemy's hands if the birds were allowed to live—but his shaking hands botched the aviancide. After several attempts, the bird was finally dead and Bertrand said, "There's been another shooting at Club Club."

"So?" asked Thimbleton, whose father and uncle and other uncle had all been murdered within the confines of that wretched establishment.

With an aged sigh, Bertrand admitted, "Headquarters is reassigning us to the Club Club shooting. They're not pleased with our progress on the Banko murder case, which, even I have to admit, is basically nonexistent."

His face burning with shame and fly bites, Thimbleton tossed his Marrowburg Steamer to the vomit-strewn ground. "What?! They can't do that to us!"

"They already have! And there's no use denying it, this is all your fault!"

"My fault?"

"Sure. I've been doing all the heavy lifting during this investigation. Every lead we've had, though they haven't really led us anywhere, has been thanks to my second sight."

"Oh really? You thought some mythical burning man shot Paulo with an arrow when he was actually choked."

"Okay, alright, I'll grant you that there are times when the second sight isn't firing on all its cylinders, but what exactly have you been doing?"

"I've been doing all the actual lifting, carrying you from place to place, even the bathroom. Super-ick! This whole day has had nothing to do with my dreams coming true, which was what was promised!"

"Oh my God, kid, you know nothing about real police work."

"That's right, I don't. And really, I shouldn't. I'm just a regular thirteen-year-old kid suffering from Progeria Syndrome, a kid who probably won't live to see his twentieth birthday, a kid who's confused and scared and really just wants to go home to his mom and dad. Today was supposed to be fun, a distraction from the shitty hand I've been dealt by Sweet Baby Geezie, but instead it's been about you and your sciatica and your glaucoma and your shriveled penis!"

Tears the size of the flies that swarmed around the two men came pouring forth from Thimbleton's eyes. He jumped from the patrol cart. His tennis shoes made a sickening *thlwarf* noise when they landed on the vomity blacktop.

"Where are you going?" demanded Bertrand.

"Sorry, Mr. Kropp, but I'm heading home. I've had enough of police work."

Bertrand snorted. "Quitting? Is that what you're doing, partner? Quitting?"

"Technically, I'm not quitting since I don't really have a job. And I don't even have a dream anymore to come true."

His hands trembling, Thimbleton pulled off his pilot wings and tossed them into the sea of vomit.

But before Thimbleton could head back to civilian life, Bertrand's frail body convulsed and he shouted, "I'm having one, I'm having one of my bouts of second sight. I can see Paulo being throttled by a dolphin-riding–"

"No!" shouted Thimbleton, spittle flying. "You can't see a darn thing because you don't have second sight! You never did! All this talk about seeing things is just a stupid lie and I'm sick of it!"

Bertrand watched the old-looking young man stomp away from Big Black's Hut of Steaming Entrails' parking lot, his head hanging like a condemned man.

Chapter Fifteen

Big Black's Hut of Steaming Entrails Redux

Ten minutes earlier, Ram, sitting in Big Black's parking lot was enjoying his third Marrowburg Steamer while the baby gangster strapped in the back of the lilac Dodge Aspire could only watch him eat, drool, and file complaints. "C'mon, you fatass, give me just one bite!"

Afraid Jaydon could choke, Ram wouldn't allow the baby his own hot dog from Big Black's Hut of Steaming Entrails. Jaydon sat in his car seat, sucking on ketchup packets.

"Sorry, boss, but hot dogs are like the number one thing that babies choke on."

"How do you know such garbage?"

After a shallow shrug and a massive bite, "I read it in a book a few months back."

Infuriated, Jaydon looked out the window of the car, his bottom lip quivering in anger, his face an unhealthy shade of crimson as he strained to make a most unpleasant horsy in his pants.

But all thoughts of forced defecation disappeared when he spied, through the miasma of flies that called Big Black's their home, a patrol cart at the other end of the parking lot. On the buckboard sat two old guys, one of whom was eating, the other simply glowering. The baby gangster studied the pair of men. He didn't recognize the short one—the one devouring a hot dog—but the other one was his nemesis, Officer Bertrand Kropp.

"Sweet Baby Geezie, ain't that guy retired yet?"

"What?" asked Ram. Per usual he was oblivious to the surrounding world while his mouth was stuffed with steaming entrails and pudding.

Sinking down in his baby seat, Jaydon warned, "We got company, bad company. A pair of coppers."

Instinctively, the brute ducked down, bringing his Marrowburg Steamer with him. Slowly swiveling his perfectly spherical head, Ram spotted the patrol cart, recognizing Kropp but not the new guy who was obviously an old guy.

Taking another bite, Ram watched as a police carrier pigeon descended from the smoggy heavens and landed squarely on Kropp's bald head. Taking his sweet time, the old cop retrieved the carrier pigeon, his hands veiny and shaking. After reading the message printed on the pigeon's stomach, he cruelly and slowly wrung the poor bird's neck. After a short, but obviously heated, discussion, the short cop threw his badge away, climbed down, and shuffled away, his head hanging low.

Officer Kropp stayed, aged tears falling from his aged eyes.

From the backseat, Jaydon giggled babyishly. "I love seeing that old fuck in pain. Okay, let's be on our way. We gotta find Ruby Redd."

After a moment, the thug said, "Really, boss? Hasn't there been enough carnage and destruction for one day?"

"You know what they say, Ram. You can never be too rich or too thin or have too much carnage and destruction."

"Do they really say that?"

Ignoring his henchman's query, Jaydon said, "You know, I've been putting a lot of thought toward this Ruby Redd issue and I think I've found the answer."

"Is that so, boss?"

"Yeah. What did Paulo tell us about Ruby Redd?"

"Can't quite recall."

"He told us that Ruby Redd wanted to have a baby, but not with me, which had forced her to find a new man. From that, we figured that whoever this fucking guy was, he was the guy who planted me. And what did we learn from Violet Greene pre-ocelot attack?"

"Ahh...."

"That she married this jerk who was rich and powerful and I couldn't touch him. Now, what did Rinky Dink tell us before you beat him to death? That despite being powerful and rich and all that, this guy couldn't have kids, right? So, if we put all of them things together, who do we have? Someone who's powerful and loved by all and can't have kids?"

"I dunno, boss."

"Well, it certainly sounds like Senator Dove to me. Sweet Baby Geezie, how could I be so blind? It all makes perfect sense when you put a little thought to it! Ruby Redd was campaigning for that reformer asshole and, obviously, she fell in love with him even though he is ball-less in the nut region. Everyone knows he got his nutsack shot off by a Commie bullet when he helped take back Grenada while serving in the Marines. Being afraid of what I would do to him when I found out about their affair, he got the jump on me and tricked me into that alley and pumped me full of lead."

"Really? After all of these clues, that's what you've come up with?"

"Yeah, like I said, it all adds up."

"Sure. So what are you going to do about it?"

"I'm gonna kill the son-of-a-bitch."

Chapter Sixteen

A Burned Globule

Having been a cop for over eight decades, Bertrand knew there was only one place to find a thirteen-year-old boy who looked ninety: the arcade at the Marrowburg Senior Center, which, due to recent budget cutbacks, was housed in the same building as the city's sewage treatment facility.

As he suspected, Bertrand found the place empty save for the dying boy. Old people hate everything, but they particularly hate arcades.

Thimbleton was playing foosball all by his lonesome, which is a tedious and time-consuming endeavor involving hitting the ball then shuffling to the other side of the table to play a little defense.

Although he had his elderly back to Bertrand when the old cop shuffled in, Thimbleton asked, "How'd you find me?"

"I came to tell you that you're right. I don't have the Gift. I don't have second sight. Never have. My whole life has been a lie. I'm sorry I wasted your day—one of your last—with all my foolishness."

"That's okay. It was kind of fun, really. Say, how did you find me?"

"It was quite easy, really. After I called headquarters and finally found someone sober enough to answer my questions, I found that you lied to me. You weren't going home to your mom and dad. You don't have a mom or a dad or a home."

Bertrand listened to the whole teary story. A few years back, Mr. and Mrs. Thimbleton felt emotionally drained by their dying son and drove out to Abattoir Ridge, clasped their hands, and jumped to their deaths. Romantic, but it didn't really benefit their ten-year-old son. He had to move into the Marrowburg Retirement Village and Ice Hockey Training Center. When Bertrand called there and finally found someone sober enough to answer his questions, he was told that the last time anyone had seen Thimbleton was that morning, when he donned his borrowed police uniform, affixed his plastic pilot wings, and told the front desk that he would never be coming back.

Studying the little plastic men on the little plastic playing field, Thimbleton sighed. "I was hoping to die in the line of duty."

Bertrand laughed, a noise that shocked the dying boy to such a degree that he spun, grabbing for his faltering heart.

The old cop explained, "I've felt that way every day for the last few decades. I get up every day and put on my uniform and strap on my gun, with the assistance of a home help aid, and go down to headquarters. You see, Thimbleton, every good cop wants to take one for the team."

"But I'm not a cop, I'm just a dying teenager adrift in this world."

"You're a cop for today, dammit!"

"And today is nearly over," said Thimbleton. He gestured toward a clock that hung crooked above a *Galaxian* game. 4:14.

"Well, okay, we're still both cops for another forty-six minutes, but I plan to make the most out of that time. Don't you want to make a difference before you die? Go out with a bang?"

"Well, I already did the sex thing. I didn't think that would ever happen–"

"I'm talking about your life as a cop. Don't you want that to also end with a bang?"

"Sure," said Thimbleton with a slight shrug.

"So do I. And neither of us has much time left, so let's head over to Club Club and ask a few pointed questions, partner. Sure, it's not solving the cool strip club owner murder, but it's all we got. And, honestly, Thimbleton, you're all I've got. In my eight decades on the force, I've had 1,455 different partners. Not one of them stuck with me for over five hours. My last partner, who I had over a decade ago, tried to kill me when I led him to the wrong abandoned warehouse. When we found the right abandoned warehouse, which contained eight dead bodies, my partner went crazy and tried to shoot me with an underwater spear gun."

"Golly, Mr. Kropp... was he thrown off the force?"

Again, Bertrand laughed heartily. "Hardly. As with nearly every Marrowburg police force investigation, there was a cover-up. My partner was given his aquatics marksman badge—though he missed me by a good three feet—and a promotion. In fact, today that man is Captain Milktwat. All I'm trying to say is that you're the best partner I've ever had, and I'm not about to lose you to a game of foosball."

Nodding slowly, Thimbleton consider this statement for a moment. "Well, I'm all out of quarters anyway."

Bertrand smiled.

Thimbleton shuffled toward the elderly cop. Looked him right in the eye and said, "Let's roll, partner."

With trembling hands, Bertrand held out Thimbleton's pilot's wings, which were still dripping with vomit. Ignoring the sick, the officer-for-a-day snatched up his version of a badge and pinned it to his chest.

Even though there'd been a bar fight that had resulted in several broken bones and three deaths (Bonnie Voyage, Pervy Claus, and some other poor son of a bitch) Club Club's business was not affected. In fact, the joint was hopping, packed with folks who didn't mind the pools of blood and the air reeking of cordite. There was a moment of discontent when members of the Marrowburg police force arrived to investigate the fatal donnybrook, but that disappeared quickly when it was discovered that the boys in blue, who'd been celebrating a charred Officer Globule's release from the burn unit, were more blotto than their drunken counterparts. Soon the assembled ne'er-do-wells and the cops were singing ribald songs and sharing drinks.

This newfound reverie was dampened, especially among the police, when Thimbleton carried Bertrand through the door. The inebriated officers jeered at the new arrivals and some threw their badges. Officer Globule, who looked like an overcooked Marrowburg Steamer, stumbled toward them, not even bothering to put his beer down. "What are you doing here, Kropp?"

"Sweet Baby Geezie," said Bertrand when he saw the blackened man, "what happened to you, Globule?"

A laugh that wasn't a laugh. "Well, here's a hint. After I get good and drunk, I'm heading off to my first Face Burned Off Anonymous meeting."

"I still... I still don't understand."

Globule sighed a burned sigh. "I got attacked by your birthday slash retirement cake, which leads me to ask again, what are you doing here? Aren't you retired?"

Slowly, Bertrand gestured toward an hourglass that was on the bar and said, "Officer-For-A-Day Thimbleton and I are on the clock for another twenty-two minutes."

Laughing and shaking his scorched head, Officer Globule headed back toward the bar. Over his shoulder, he said, "Good luck with that. We've already searched this joint, and there are no clues to be found."

"Ignore him," advised Bertrand into his partner's ear, "he's just a little put out by the cake incident. Now put me down, and do it gently, please."

The floor of the bar was a mess with blood, broken chairs, and bodies that still hadn't been removed or even covered.

But Bertrand saw it right away: the proverbial needle in the proverbial haystack. He would have shouted if his lungs were capable.

"There, partner," he whispered excitedly. "There's our clue."

Thimbleton followed his eye line and spied the small rubber object lying in the detritus. He walked over and picked it up. Turned it over in his hand, studied it.

After he made a thorough examination, Thimbleton proclaimed, "This is a pacifier, partner."

"Exactly. What's a pacifier doing in this awful joint? Let me have a look at it."

Thimbleton handed the old cop the pacifier. Bertrand saw that it was smudged with green lipstick. "There's only one person in Marrowburg who wears green lipstick... I think we should have a little talk with Violet Greene."

Chapter Seventeen

Politics Makes Strange Bedfellows

From the handful of Geezie-awful political movies that Ruby Redd had dragged him to at the Marrowburg Cineplex and Gardening Center, Jaydon knew that campaign headquarters was going to be a beehive of activity filled with well-intentioned but frazzled folks, working on little sleep and lots of caffeine, wearing half-tied ties and shirts stained with sweat, running around, barking out orders, slamming phones down. Despite the boring subject matter, it had appeared very exciting to the gangster.

Senator Dove's campaign headquarters was the exact opposite of this.

It was very quiet and as empty as the arcade at the Senior Center/Sewage Treatment Plant. There was about an acre of open floor space, with one desk manned by one old woman at the back of the room.

Smoking, she packed overstuffed files into a box haphazardly. Squinting at the brute and the baby through her personal fug, she said, "If you two fucks are looking for the childcare slash lumber mill, it's down the block."

Jaydon spoke, employing his indoor voice: "Oh, no. No lumber for us. We're here to volunteer for Senator Dove. We think he has some real neat ideas about political things and stuff."

Spitting the cigarette onto the linoleum and crushing it with an orthopedic sneaker, the old woman cackled cancerously, "You're a little late, aren't you, boys? Senator Dove got re-elected five months ago."

"Of course," said the baby gangster, "everything has changed while I was in womb jail."

81

The old woman was the midst of scorching another coffin nail when she heard the words "womb jail." This caused her to kill the lighter and glare at the baby with a beard. "What the fuck did you just say, little man?"

"Nothing, ma'am. So where does one find the great Senator Dove these days? Washington DC, I assume."

"Oh no, the poor man suffers from domeophobia, which, I'm sure you're aware, is the fear of domes. Washington DC is like his version of hell. He spends most of his time with us little folks right here in Marrowburg."

"I bet he does," hissed Jaydon, thinking of the reformer senator getting bestial atop his girlfriend. "Okay, so where can we find him specifically, like right now? Does he have an office or something?"

"Not really. He works out of his Yugo, which is usually hard to find. But you're in luck, he's giving a speech down at the Calvin Coolidge Assassination Fun Park this evening at six. It's gonna be a real doozy. He's talking about cleaning up the city and crap like that."

"Yes, it will certainly be a doozy," promised Jaydon, thinking about how many orifices he was going to add to the senator's body.

Chapter Eighteen

The Danger of an Escaped Ocelot

With every step, Officer-For-A-Day Thimbleton's back cried out in agony. Not only because of his Progeria Syndrome, but the young man had also wrenched it during some acrobatic and educational sex with the faux Margaret Sanger. Not to mention that he was carrying his aged partner up several flights of stairs.

Between gasps of breath, Thimbleton asked, "Why are we here again?"

"Violet Greene was at Club Club during the shooting," said Bertrand. "She might be able to tell us something." But he had no real hope of this happening. The interview was going to be a dead end just like all the other dead ends that had plagued his career. He only had a few minutes left in his life as a cop and he was certain he was going to spend them chasing his tail. How fitting.

They arrived on the third floor of the Gristle Arms to find Violet Greene's door open wide.

"It's as if she were expecting us," wheezed Bertrand, who was out of breath even though he hadn't walked a step all day.

"I don't have a good feeling about this," wheezed Thimbleton.

"I thought you didn't believe in second sight."

Chuckling, Thimbleton carried the old cop across the threshold as if they were the most unlikely married couple in the history of matrimony.

The carnage that awaited them was a real kick in the sciatic nerve. Scattered all around the living room were chunks of what had once been Violet Greene. An arm here, a vulva there. Blood stained every surface, even the ceiling. Stretched out on the couch was an ocelot, rabid and contented. It languidly cleaned bits of face and blood off its beautiful coat.

The creature stopped cleaning and eyed the cops. The cops stopped walking and eyed the creature. The room was so quiet that if any of the three of them would have been in possession of a pin and, for some reason, dropped said pin, it would have rung out like a shot.

It was Thimbleton who broke this bizarro still-life tableau. His first move was to drop Bertrand like a sack of moldy potatoes. Being a lifelong cop, the old man obeyed all laws, including those governed by gravity, and he fell toward the floor. This blur of gray made the ocelot leap to his feet, growling rabidly. Coiling its inner springs, the beast readied to pounce.

Before Bertrand even finished his journey to the floor—an act which would break both his hips, both his arms, both his legs, and a cageful of ribs—Thimbleton had his hand on his piece, a .38 that Captain Milktwat had loaned him.

It suddenly occurred to him that he hadn't even considered if the weapon was loaded. Normally, he was certain, any police force with a modicum of common sense would never arm a visiting kid dying of Progeria Syndrome, but this was Marrowburg after all.

At least that was Thimbleton's hope. His last hope.

Even though his rapidly aging hands were trembling, the officer-for-a-day drew his weapon and leveled it at the ocelot, locking eyes with the creature.

The beast leapt, coming at Thimbleton and his wrinkled but still edible face like a stripped and spotted freight train. The dying boy, who didn't want to die, desperately wished to scream but could find no breath left in his failing body.

Fearing that he might never breathe again, Thimbleton pulled the trigger. Fortuitously, the .38 was loaded. Also fortuitous: the bullet found its mark, striking the flying ocelot square in the chest, canceling his dinner plans. The wounded creature fell from the air like a paperweight that would be impractical due to its size and rabidness and landed on its side on the already bloody floor, right next to Bertrand. Though suffering from a multitude of broken bones and having just nearly been devoured by a rabid ocelot, Bertrand was feeling no pain. In fact, he was smiling, his eyes brimming with tears of joy. A wave of pleasure washed over the shores of his soul.

He could see things... everything. Vivid images filled the theatre in his mind. Knocking on death's door, he found he did, in fact, have the Gift. In his second sight, he saw Ram Bountybar carry a baby into Paulo Banko's office. Bertrand knew he'd seen this baby before in his life but couldn't place him. Everything about the baby was familiar: the five o'clock shadow, his I (HEART) SNATCH tattoo, and smirk, but none of it added up. Not until the baby spoke in a gruff voice, threatening Paulo. Now it all made sense, even though it was impossible. The baby was Kid Phoenix. Bertrand watched as Ram stuck the rattle down poor Paulo's throat. Deeper and deeper.

Then Bertrand's mind slipped a gear and went into the future. He saw the evil baby gangster brandishing a gun in a crowd in the Calvin Coolidge Assassination Fun Park, trying to aim the weapon at a rotund man standing at a podium that was caked with red, white, and blue bunting.

Then everything went black, bland. Returned to normal.

Bertrand's eyes snapped open and he gasped for air. He was shivering while every pore in his body was working overtime in the sweat department.

For the first time in his life, a real vision had struck Bertrand Kropp and the experience scared the hell out of him.

When his eyes finally focused, he found he was face-to-face with Officer-For-A-Day Thimbleton, who was kneeling over him.

"Sweet Baby Geezie, Mr. Kropp," panted the dying kid, who looked like he'd aged ten years in the past ten seconds. "I thought I'd lost you there. It looked like you were having a heart attack or something. You were babbling in some strange language and twitching real weird. It was super scary."

Bertrand smiled up at his partner. "I just experienced the Gift."

"Oh, Mr. Kropp, we've talked about this. You know you don't have–"

"It showed me who killed Paulo Banko."

"Who?" asked Thimbleton, still skeptical.

"Kid Phoenix."

"But Kid Phoenix is dead."

"Yes, he was shot outside Stripping Through History, but apparently it didn't take. He's back from the grave as a baby and he's as mad as hell."

"Back from the grave? That don't make no sense."

"This is Marrowburg, partner. Nothing makes no sense. We have to stop that evil baby."

"I don't know, Mr. Kropp, I should be taking you to the hospital."

"Fuck the hospital, Officer Thimbleton. According to my vision, we have to get to the Calvin Coolidge Assassination Fun Park before Kid Phoenix does. He's going to kill Senator Dove."

Chapter Nineteen

Death at the Death Pavilion

In 1901, after the McKinley assassination really put Buffalo on the map, the fine residents of Marrowburg desperately wished for their very own presidential assassination. The horrible, bloody death of a local politician just wouldn't do, as they tended to get murdered left and right. Not a week passed without some unfortunate ombudsman taking a knife to the gonads or worse. It had to be a national politician.

The main drawback of this curious display of civic pride was that no one of any note ever came within a hundred miles of the city limits of Marrowburg. The nearest thing to a presidential visit was when Ulysses S. Grant's personal ottoman maker passed through Marrowburg on the train whilst escaping an angry wife (not his own) and he didn't even bother to disembark the train during the whistle stop. He just peed out the window.

In a desperate bid to secure re-election in 1921, a local enterprising dogcatcher named Hugo Shrunk announced that his old friend Calvin Coolidge was coming to Marrowburg to campaign for him.

Of course, Shrunk didn't really know Coolidge and had never clapped eyes on the man, but that didn't matter. He simply found a local bum who bore a passing resemblance to Silent Cal, liquored him up, dressed him in some shoddy finery, and dragged him to a campaign speech. Within seconds of this ersatz Coolidge taking the stage, he was struck by seven bullets from three different guns and died on the spot. The dog catcher, now considered a local hero, won re-election in a landslide, but, ironically, was mauled to death by a rabid ocelot a few weeks later while skinny-dipping with Miss Teenage Marrowburg, who survived the attack but had a majority of her beard gnawed off.

The ruse of the Coolidge assassination has been maintained until this day due to the fact that television reception in Marrowburg is poor at best, the bulk of the general population are illiterate, and those that do read tend to stick with pornography. Recently, there had been some rumors surfacing that the person buried in Marrowburg's Evergreen Cemetery and Impound Lot was not the president like his gravestone claimed, but those tales were quickly squashed by some civic-minded fists.

Niggling doubts aside, Marrowburgites loved their questionable hometown presidential assassination and proved this love by donating tens of thousands of dollars (and a few chickens) to build the Calvin Coolidge Assassination Fun Park. The respect for this institution was obvious—unlike so many other struggling Marrowburg businesses, it didn't have to share its space with other businesses; the fun park was wholly unto itself.

And wholly fun. While at the park, a family could take a chance, literally, on the River of Blood log flume or cross their fingers and dine on Bullet Burgers in the Smokin' Gun Food Court (where the best case scenario, health-wise, was a nasty case of halitosis) or they could ride the world's only roller coast made completely out of cow bones: the Death Express. Thanks to the Tunnel of Gloves—where each boater received an oar and a prophylactic, both of which were hastily discarded into the brackish water—over sixty percent of Marrowburgites claimed to have been conceived at the Calvin Coolidge Assassination Fun Park.

But Jaydon wasn't looking for a nasty case of halitosis or to get his baby rocks off. He was looking for Senator Dove, and as he was carried into the fun park, his tiny, rapidly beating heart was filled with malice and forethought, and his diaper was filled with something just as putrid.

Dove was easy to find. Jaydon just ordered Ram to follow the overflowing crowd, who were all heading toward the Death Pavilion in the back of the park. The excitement in the air was palatable as proud Marrowburgites were showing up in scores, hoping to be on hand for a little political bloodshed. Watching a senator get gunned down would certainly not be as historic or cool as watching a president eat lead, but it was still something to do with the kids on a Friday night.

With all the foolish reforms Dove was promising—such as forcing children to ride only on the *inside* of school buses, no longer using chickens as cash, no more sock guns—the local bookies were giving 5 to 2 odds that tonight was the night that the vast Marrowburg underground would rise up and slaughter this forward-thinking and nutless politician.

Bertrand also wasn't looking for halitosis or nooky when he was carried into the Calvin Coolidge Assassination Fun Park just seconds after Jaydon arrived—he was looking for Kid Phoenix reincarnated. Swept along with the throng, the old cop searched for a suspicious-looking baby. Unfortunately, there were a staggering number of infants being carried into the fun park. Even if Senator Dove wasn't gunned down this evening, it's a tradition in Marrowburg to have one's baby kissed by politicians in hopes that the little nipper gets an STD, which always leads to heaps of hush money.

Upon entering the Death Pavilion, which was also fashioned from cow bones, Jaydon spied a small stage in the corner. And up on that stage, in all his fat and sweaty glory, was Senator Dove, doing all the usual things politicians do that make people want to shoot them: waving his pudgy arms and making pudgy promises. Not that anyone in the crowd was listening; they were simply waiting patiently for a little gunplay to come along to brighten their dreary, little lives.

Drooling with bad intent and kicking feistily, Jaydon ordered his henchman to hand over his gun.

"But, boss... your tiny little hands."

"Hand it over or I'll use it on you."

Reaching deep into his coat, Ram pulled out his .44. As carefully as he could, he placed it in the tiny, soft hands of the baby.

"Now get me close to that stage. Push people to the ground if you have to, you stupid hunk of beef."

Putting his shoulder down, which reminded him of his gridiron days, Ram did as he was told, knocking folks and chickens out of the way, which left a wake of swearing and aggravated cackling.

It was this disturbance, this massive rippling through the packed, bloodthirsty crowd, that alerted Bertrand to the reincarnated gangster's location.

"Notice, Officer-For-A-Day Thimbleton, where the crowd is parting. Take me there!"

Apologizing and flashing his pilot's wings to silence the dirty stares, the faux cop did as he was told.

The brute and the armed baby were drawing nearer to the stage. Excited, Jaydon kicked and wriggled with such ferocity that Ram nearly fumbled the squirming flesh football.

About ten feet shy of the stage, the pair ran into a solid black and white wall. Nuns, a whole flock of them. If you're familiar with brides of the Baby Geezie, you know they never budge. On anything. Especially if you've ever attempted to talk one into a sex act.

Uncomfortable with simply bowling them over, Ram begged the nuns' pardons. To their stiff backs. Only one deigned to turn around. This nun, despite the austere, tit-obscuring habit, was striking looking. She locked eyes with Ram as her jaw dropped.

Jaydon stopped kicking, ceased squirming. It was the same nun he'd spied outside the Face Burned Off Anonymous meeting at St. Jude Catholic Church and Recycling Center. The one with wisps of flaming hair and emerald eyes. The one he mistook for Ruby Redd. But now that he was close enough to smell her, close enough to reach out and touch her, no amount of nunness could obscure the fact that this woman was, amazingly, the beautiful and haunting Ruby Redd.

Her thick lips—which looked so strange without her bright red lipstick—parted. She searched for something to say, but didn't find it. Time passed, but Jaydon couldn't say how much—a minute, an hour—as they don't make watches for babies.

Finally, the woman found her nun tongue, "Oh, lover... I was... I was hoping I'd never see you again...."

"Look me in the eye when you're talking to me, you two-timing bitch!" spat the baby, bubbles of pure hate forming on his lips. All thoughts of gunning down the Senator had departed.

Sister Ruby Redd gasped when she looked down upon the bearded baby. Her eyes went even wider and she could only find one usable word in her vocabulary. "Kid?"

Though equipped with only a tiny baby brain, realization washed over Jaydon. His old girlfriend wasn't referring to him as "lover." She was looking at, speaking to, getting all gooey over Ram Bountybar.

Looking back and forth between his dumb-as-an-unloaded gun henchman and the most beautiful woman he'd ever banged, Jaydon couldn't fucking believe it.

The baby pointed his words and the .44 at the man who was holding him. "You fucking fuck! This is why you dragged your feet all day... why you didn't want to find who killed me. This is why you dragged Rinky Dink away from me so I couldn't hear what he was saying. And that travel agent, talking about that romantic trip nine months ago. She was talking to you, not me. You're the man Ruby Redd threw me aside for. That's why you had a baby seat and a Bjorn and all that stupid baby knowledge! You two were going to have a kid together! Sweet Baby Geezie! I trusted you with my life and you stabbed me in the back with bullets!"

The crowd around them backed away, formed a circle. Tingling, some giggling, they'd found the gunplay that they'd prayed for.

Thrusting his arms toward the bony ceiling of the Death Pavilion, the brute dropped Jaydon. Ass over unformed fontanel, the baby tumbled through the air. Landing badly and crying out, the lil' gangster managed to hold onto the gun, which dwarfed him.

"Say your prayers, you two-timing asshole," wailed Jaydon, aiming.

"Listen, boss, I'll admit, some of the stuff you said was true. I did steal your girlfriend."

Stepping forward, Ruby Redd offered, "Oh hell, he didn't steal me. I'm not a bag of gold, I'm a person. I went willingly. I had to leave because of the way you treated me."

"Yeah," said Ram, "you have really poor management skills."

He'd learned such language while working at Dead Cow Burger Joint.

The nun continued, "You'd stay out all night, chasing other skirts, hitting me if I questioned your behavior. I wanted to have a child, not date one. At first, Ram was just a shoulder to cry on... then I moved my head a little lower."

Jaydon couldn't believe what he was hearing. His head was spinning like a bullet traveling down the barrel of a gun. "So you two bumped me off just to get me out of the way?"

"I didn't have nothing to do with that," vowed the nun. "When I found out that you'd been shot, I knew it was Ram who'd done you in and that he done it for me. I couldn't handle that. So I went into hiding. I got myself to a nunnery and became a bride of the Sweet Baby Geezie."

"Of course," whispered Jaydon. "You married someone powerful, someone everybody loves, someone I could never touch: the Baby Geezie."

"Yes, I had to pay for my sins: I loved the man who killed the man who loved me."

"That ain't exactly how it went down," interjected Ram. "It's true that I was the one who sent Rinky Dink for you. I was the one who wanted to meet you in the alley behind Stripping Through History, but I only wanted to talk, to tell you the truth, to work things out. But when you stepped out of the door of the strip club, a third person stepped from the shadows and drilled you in the back."

"Who?" Jaydon could sense that the big man was telling the truth. He was still planning on shooting Ram for pouring the steaming cobs to his gal, but apparently he still had other people on his plate to kill.

"I dunno. Once the shooting started, I got out of there. I didn't know what to do. So after I called the cops, I went to the hospital and tanning center and watched you die. That was the worst night of my life. Sure, I wanted your girl, but I didn't want you dead. You was my best friend. Didn't I prove that today? Carrying you around everyplace, changing you poopy diapers, helping you look for your murderer?"

"You weren't helping me," said Jaydon. "You was helping yourself. You lied to me about what Rinky Dink said in that alley, tried to pin my murder on Semple Skehill."

Ram hung his head. "Yeah, I was just scared Rinky Dink would tell you about me and Ruby Redd. I panicked. Just like that night you got plugged. After the hospital, I ran all the way to Ruby Redd's apartment in the rain, but she'd already disappeared. So I disappeared too. I moved to the suburbs and got a job at Dead Cow Burger Joint since I didn't know who killed you and I thought my life might have been in danger."

"I did," called a frail voice from behind the bizarre love triangle. "And it is."

Everyone turned. Standing at the edge of the edgy crowd were two police officers. Bertrand, who was cradled by the other old cop, had his weapon out and trained on the baby.

For a moment a hungry silence filled the pavilion. Even the politician, forgotten, shut the hell up.

Finally, Jaydon asked, "What the fuck are you talking about, old man?"

"I mean," said Bertrand, his voice gaining strength, "that I was the one who killed you."

Officer-For-A-Day Thimbleton shook his head. "What? Why?"

"Because Kid Phoenix was an arrogant hoodlum who got away with every crime he ever committed. For years I'd been trying to catch him and I couldn't, despite my second sight. I just wanted to accomplish something before I died. Go out with a bang!"

"So you just gunned him down in cold blood?" Thimbleton asked, aghast.

"I did, and I'm proud of it."

Thimbleton said, "In all my minutes of being a cop, I've never heard anything more disgusting." "I think I'll just–"

But the world would never know what Officer-For-A-Day Thimbleton was planning—perhaps he was thinking about purchasing a strawberry Murder Cone or playing a game of Hide the Evidence—because, at that very moment, he suffered a massive coronary. Grabbing his chest, he dropped Bertrand, who would have broken some bones if he hadn't already done that.

With a partial groan, Thimbleton fell to the floor, dead. Landed near Bertrand, who stared daggers at Jaydon. "That's it, you killed my partner!"

"I believe, technically, it was you who killed your partner," Jaydon said, talking to stall for time. He was moving around the .44, trying to get a bead on the cop, but it was rather difficult with his tiny baby hands.

"Whatever. I'm gonna kill you again, Kid Phoenix!"

"His name," roared Ram, "is Jaydon!"

On his tree-trunky legs, the man took a few steps toward the ancient cop. It was a foolish move and one filled with lead. Even though his arm was broken and his hand was trembling, Bertrand put one, two, three nasty holes in Ram's chest.

The brute dropped to the floor of the pavilion, dead.

There was a smattering of applause from the crowd and one very pained scream from Ruby Redd. Tears streaming, the nun ran to where the big man had fallen. With no concern for staining her tit-obscuring habit, she pulled Ram's bloody body to her chest and rocked back and forth, patting his bald head and whispering sweet nothings in his dead ear.

Glaucoma-y eyes flashing, Bertrand looked around wildly at the assembled crowd. "You all saw, you saw that I had to do it. The brute was gonna bash my brains in."

"Now that's my job," said Ruby Redd, as cold as a frosted pane. As if she were putting a baby down for a nap, the nun gently placed Ram's head back on the floor. She stood—tall, elegant, severe—beginning a slow march toward Bertrand, filled with malice and forethought.

"Don't make me shoot you," threatened the old cop. "I will, you know. I'll–" But the world would never find out exactly what Officer Kropp had up his sleeve. For at that very moment, he suffered a massive coronary. Dropping his still smoking gun, he grabbed his hundred-year-old chest and groaned his last earthly groan. He would have fallen to the floor if he hadn't already made the trip.

With both officers down and no one left to crush the crowd's dreams, they went crazy. There were cheers, hoots, and the Marrowburg tradition of tossing several children toward the ceiling with no thought of catching them.

Still crying, Ruby Redd turned to face Jaydon.

Maneuvering the heavy weapon, the baby said, "I ought to shoot you right between your lying eyes."

"You ought to."

From the stage, Senator Dove piped up, "See, folks, this is exactly what I'm talking about up here. We don't need such violence in Marrowburg We need—"

Not that the world really cared, but it would never find out exactly what Dove was going to do about violence, because three shots rang out like the Liberty Bell through the pavilion.

The baby gangster had put the politician in his grave.

Now those assembled really went off their collective nut, hugging each other, strangers kissing strangers.

With a bemused smile, Ruby Redd sauntered toward Jaydon, her hips keeping time with the universe.

With great difficulty, the baby re-aimed the .44, right at the nun's obscured boobs. "Nothing would give me greater pleasure right now that to blow you away."

"But you're not going to do that." She kept sauntering, another small smile blooming on her beautiful face.

"Why not?"

"Because you're my good little baby."

Reaching down and grasping the warm gun, Ruby Redd flung it into the crowd to give them a souvenir. Clutching the neck of her habit, the nun pulled downward with all her might. Ripping the fabric, she ridded her boobs of their obscurity. With maternal arms, she picked up the disarmed baby and brought him to her nipple. Milk and tears flowed as she turned toward the door of the pavilion. The crowd parted and no one said a word as the pair exited the building. A fucking Madonna and child.

Bix Skahill is.

BIZARRO BOOKS

CATALOG   SPRING 2013

ERASERHEAD PRESS

Your major resource for the bizarro fiction genre:

WWW.BIZARROCENTRAL.COM

Introduce yourselves to the bizarro fiction genre and all of its authors with the Bizarro Starter Kit series. Each volume features short novels and short stories by ten of the leading bizarro authors, designed to give you a perfect sampling of the genre for only $10.

BB-0X1
"The Bizarro Starter Kit" (Orange)

Featuring D. Harlan Wilson, Carlton Mellick III, Jeremy Robert Johnson, Kevin L Donihe, Gina Ranalli, Andre Duza, Vincent W. Sakowski, Steve Beard, John Edward Lawson, and Bruce Taylor. **236 pages $10**

BB-0X2
"The Bizarro Starter Kit" (Blue)

Featuring Ray Fracalossy, Jeremy C. Shipp, Jordan Krall, Mykle Hansen, Andersen Prunty, Eckhard Gerdes, Bradley Sands, Steve Aylett, Christian TeBordo, and Tony Rauch. **244 pages $10**

BB-0X2
"The Bizarro Starter Kit" (Purple)

Featuring Russell Edson, Athena Villaverde, David Agranoff, Matthew Revert, Andrew Goldfarb, Jeff Burk, Garrett Cook, Kris Saknussemm, Cody Goodfellow, and Cameron Pierce **264 pages $10**

BB-001"The Kafka Effekt" D. Harlan Wilson — A collection of forty-four irreal short stories loosely written in the vein of Franz Kafka, with more than a pinch of William S. Burroughs sprinkled on top. **211 pages $14**

BB-002 "Satan Burger" Carlton Mellick III — The cult novel that put Carlton Mellick III on the map ... Six punks get jobs at a fast food restaurant owned by the devil in a city violently overpopulated by surreal alien cultures. **236 pages $14**

BB-003 "Some Things Are Better Left Unplugged" Vincent Sakwoski — Join The Man and his Nemesis, the obese tabby, for a nightmare roller coaster ride into this postmodern fantasy. **152 pages $10**

BB-005 "Razor Wire Pubic Hair" Carlton Mellick III — A genderless humandildo is purchased by a razor dominatrix and brought into her nightmarish world of bizarre sex and mutilation. **176 pages $11**

BB-007 "The Baby Jesus Butt Plug" Carlton Mellick III — Using clones of the Baby Jesus for anal sex will be the hip sex fetish of the future. **92 pages $10**

BB-010 "The Menstruating Mall" Carlton Mellick III — "The Breakfast Club meets Chopping Mall as directed by David Lynch." - Brian Keene **212 pages $12**

BB-011 "Angel Dust Apocalypse" Jeremy Robert Johnson — Meth-heads, man-made monsters, and murderous Neo-Nazis. "Seriously amazing short stories..." - Chuck Palahniuk, author of Fight Club **184 pages $11**

BB-015 "Foop!" Chris Genoa — Strange happenings are going on at Dactyl, Inc, the world's first and only time travel tourism company.
"A surreal pie in the face!" - Christopher Moore **300 pages $14**

BB-032 **"Extinction Journals" Jeremy Robert Johnson** — An uncanny voyage across a newly nuclear America where one man must confront the problems associated with loneliness, insane dieties, radiation, love, and an ever-evolving cockroach suit with a mind of its own. **104 pages $10**

BB-037 **"The Haunted Vagina" Carlton Mellick III** — It's difficult to love a woman whose vagina is a gateway to the world of the dead. **132 pages $10**

BB-043 **"War Slut" Carlton Mellick III** — Part "1984," part "Waiting for Godot," and part action horror video game adaptation of John Carpenter's "The Thing." **116 pages $10**

BB-047 **"Sausagey Santa" Carlton Mellick III** — A bizarro Christmas tale featuring Santa as a piratey mutant with a body made of sausages. 124 pages $10

BB-048 **"Misadventures in a Thumbnail Universe" Vincent Sakowski** — Dive deep into the surreal and satirical realms of neo-classical Blender Fiction, filled with television shoes and flesh-filled skies. **120 pages $10**

BB-053 **"Ballad of a Slow Poisoner" Andrew Goldfarb** — Millford Mutterwurst sat down on a Tuesday to take his afternoon tea, and made the unpleasant discovery that his elbows were becoming flatter. **128 pages $10**

BB-055 **"Help! A Bear is Eating Me" Mykle Hansen** — The bizarro, heartwarming, magical tale of poor planning, hubris and severe blood loss...
150 pages $11

BB-056 **"Piecemeal June" Jordan Krall** — A man falls in love with a living sex doll, but with love comes danger when her creator comes after her with crab-squid assassins. **90 pages $9**

BB-058 "The Overwhelming Urge" Andersen Prunty — A collection of bizarro tales by Andersen Prunty. **150 pages $11**

BB-059 "Adolf in Wonderland" Carlton Mellick III — A dreamlike adventure that takes a young descendant of Adolf Hitler's design and sends him down the rabbit hole into a world of imperfection and disorder. **180 pages $11**

BB-061 "Ultra Fuckers" Carlton Mellick III — Absurdist suburban horror about a couple who enter an upper middle class gated community but can't find their way out. **108 pages $9**

BB-062 "House of Houses" Kevin L. Donihe — An odd man wants to marry his house. Unfortunately, all of the houses in the world collapse at the same time in the Great House Holocaust. Now he must travel to House Heaven to find his departed fiancee. **172 pages $11**

BB-064 "Squid Pulp Blues" Jordan Krall — In these three bizarro-noir novellas, the reader is thrown into a world of murderers, drugs made from squid parts, deformed gun-toting veterans, and a mischievous apocalyptic donkey. **204 pages $12**

BB-065 "Jack and Mr. Grin" Andersen Prunty — "When Mr. Grin calls you can hear a smile in his voice. Not a warm and friendly smile, but the kind that seizes your spine in fear. You don't need to pay your phone bill to hear it. That smile is in every line of Prunty's prose." - Tom Bradley. **208 pages $12**

BB-066 "Cybernetrix" Carlton Mellick III — What would you do if your normal everyday world was slowly mutating into the video game world from Tron? **212 pages $12**

BB-072 "Zerostrata" Andersen Prunty — Hansel Nothing lives in a tree house, suffers from memory loss, has a very eccentric family, and falls in love with a woman who runs naked through the woods every night. **144 pages $11**

BB-073 "The Egg Man" Carlton Mellick III — It is a world where humans reproduce like insects. Children are the property of corporations, and having an enormous ten-foot brain implanted into your skull is a grotesque sexual fetish. Mellick's industrial urban dystopia is one of his darkest and grittiest to date. **184 pages $11**

BB-074 "Shark Hunting in Paradise Garden" Cameron Pierce — A group of strange humanoid religious fanatics travel back in time to the Garden of Eden to discover it is invested with hundreds of giant flying maneating sharks. **150 pages $10**

BB-075 "Apeshit" Carlton Mellick III - Friday the 13th meets Visitor Q. Six hipster teens go to a cabin in the woods inhabited by a deformed killer. An incredibly fucked-up parody of B-horror movies with a bizarro slant. **192 pages $12**

BB-076 "Fuckers of Everything on the Crazy Shitting Planet of the Vomit At smosphere" Mykle Hansen - Three bizarro satires. Monster Cocks, Journey to the Center of Agnes Cuddlebottom, and Crazy Shitting Planet. **228 pages $12**

BB-077 "The Kissing Bug" Daniel Scott Buck — In the tradition of Roald Dahl, Tim Burton, and Edward Gorey, comes this bizarro anti-war children's story about a bohemian conenose kissing bug who falls in love with a human woman. **116 pages $10**

BB-078 "MachoPoni" Lotus Rose — It's My Little Pony... *Bizarro* style! A long time ago Poniworld was split in two. On one side of the Jagged Line is the Pastel Kingdom, a magical land of music, parties, and positivity. On the other side of the Jagged Line is Dark Kingdom inhabited by an army of undead ponies. **148 pages $11**

BB-079 "The Faggiest Vampire" Carlton Mellick III — A Roald Dahl-esque children's story about two faggy vampires who partake in a mustache competition to find out which one is truly the faggiest. **104 pages $10**

BB-080 "Sky Tongues" Gina Ranalli — The autobiography of Sky Tongues, the biracial hermaphrodite actress with tongues for fingers. Follow her strange life story as she rises from freak to fame. **204 pages $12**

BB-081 **"Washer Mouth" Kevin L. Donihe** - A washing machine becomes human and pursues his dream of meeting his favorite soap opera star. **244 pages $11**

BB-082 **"Shatnerquake" Jeff Burk** - All of the characters ever played by William Shatner are suddenly sucked into our world. Their mission: hunt down and destroy the real William Shatner. **100 pages $10**

BB-083 **"The Cannibals of Candyland" Carlton Mellick III** - There exists a race of cannibals that are made of candy. They live in an underground world made out of candy. One man has dedicated his life to killing them all. **170 pages $11**

BB-084 **"Slub Glub in the Weird World of the Weeping Willows" Andrew Goldfarb** - The charming tale of a blue glob named Slub Glub who helps the weeping willows whose tears are flooding the earth. There are also hyenas, ghosts, and a voodoo priest **100 pages $10**

BB-085 **"Super Fetus" Adam Pepper** - Try to abort this fetus and he'll kick your ass! **104 pages $10**

BB-086 **"Fistful of Feet" Jordan Krall** - A bizarro tribute to spaghetti westerns, featuring Cthulhu-worshipping Indians, a woman with four feet, a crazed gunman who is obsessed with sucking on candy, Syphilis-ridden mutants, sexually transmitted tattoos, and a house devoted to the freakiest fetishes. **228 pages $12**

BB-087 **"Ass Goblins of Auschwitz" Cameron Pierce** - It's Monty Python meets Nazi exploitation in a surreal nightmare as can only be imagined by Bizarro author Cameron Pierce. **104 pages $10**

BB-088 **"Silent Weapons for Quiet Wars" Cody Goodfellow** - "This is high-end psychological surrealist horror meets bottom-feeding low-life crime in a techno-thrilling science fiction world full of Lovecraft and magic..." -John Skipp **212 pages $12**

BB-089 "Warrior Wolf Women of the Wasteland" Carlton Mellick III — Road Warrior Werewolves versus McDonaldland Mutants...post-apocalyptic fiction has never been quite like this. **316 pages $13**

BB-091 "Super Giant Monster Time" Jeff Burk — A tribute to choose your own adventures and Godzilla movies. Will you escape the giant monsters that are rampaging the fuck out of your city and shit? Or will you join the mob of alien-controlled punk rockers causing chaos in the streets? What happens next depends on you. **188 pages $12**

BB-092 "Perfect Union" Cody Goodfellow — "Cronenberg's THE FLY on a grand scale: human/insect gene-spliced body horror, where the human hive politics are as shocking as the gore." -John Skipp. **272 pages $13**

BB-093 "Sunset with a Beard" Carlton Mellick III — 14 stories of surreal science fiction. **200 pages $12**

BB-094 "My Fake War" Andersen Prunty — The absurd tale of an unlikely soldier forced to fight a war that, quite possibly, does not exist. It's Rambo meets Waiting for Godot in this subversive satire of American values and the scope of the human imagination. **128 pages $11**

BB-095 "Lost in Cat Brain Land" Cameron Pierce — Sad stories from a surreal world. A fascist mustache, the ghost of Franz Kafka, a desert inside a dead cat. Primordial entities mourn the death of their child. The desperate serve tea to mysterious creatures. A hopeless romantic falls in love with a pterodactyl. And much more. **152 pages $11**

BB-096 "The Kobold Wizard's Dildo of Enlightenment +2" Carlton Mellick III — A Dungeons and Dragons parody about a group of people who learn they are only made up characters in an AD&D campaign and must find a way to resist their nerdy teenaged players and retarded dungeon master in order to survive. 232 **pages $12**

BB-098 "A Hundred Horrible Sorrows of Ogner Stump" Andrew Goldfarb — Goldfarb's acclaimed comic series. A magical and weird journey into the horrors of everyday life. **164 pages $11**

BB-099 "Pickled Apocalypse of Pancake Island" Cameron Pierce—A demented fairy tale about a pickle, a pancake, and the apocalypse. **102 pages $8**

BB-100 "Slag Attack" Andersen Prunty— Slag Attack features four visceral, noir stories about the living, crawling apocalypse. A slag is what survivors are calling the slug-like maggots raining from the sky, burrowing inside people, and hollowing out their flesh and their sanity. **148 pages $11**

BB-101 "Slaughterhouse High" Robert Devereaux—A place where schools are built with secret passageways, rebellious teens get zippers installed in their mouths and genitals, and once a year, on that special night, one couple is slaughtered and the bits of their bodies are kept as souvenirs. **304 pages $13**

BB-102 "The Emerald Burrito of Oz" John Skipp & Marc Levinthal —OZ IS REAL! Magic is real! The gate is really in Kansas! And America is finally allowing Earth tourists to visit this weird-ass, mysterious land. But when Gene of Los Angeles heads off for summer vacation in the Emerald City, little does he know that a war is brewing...a war that could destroy both worlds. **280 pages $13**

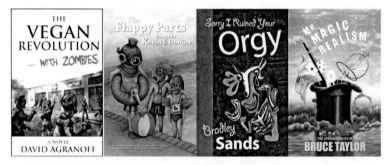

BB-103 "The Vegan Revolution... with Zombies" David Agranoff — When there's no more meat in hell, the vegans will walk the earth. **160 pages $11**

BB-104 "The Flappy Parts" Kevin L Donihe—Poems about bunnies, LSD, and police abuse. You know, things that matter. 132 **pages $11**

BB-105 "Sorry I Ruined Your Orgy" Bradley Sands—Bizarro humorist Bradley Sands returns with one of the strangest, most hilarious collections of the year. **130 pages $11**

BB-106 "Mr. Magic Realism" Bruce Taylor—Like Golden Age science fiction comics written by Freud, *Mr. Magic Realism* is a strange, insightful adventure that spans the furthest reaches of the galaxy, exploring the hidden caverns in the hearts and minds of men, women, aliens, and biomechanical cats. **152 pages $11**

BB-107 **"Zombies and Shit" Carlton Mellick III**—"Battle Royale" meets "Return of the Living Dead." Mellick's bizarro tribute to the zombie genre. **308 pages $13**

BB-108 **"The Cannibal's Guide to Ethical Living" Mykle Hansen**—Over a five star French meal of fine wine, organic vegetables and human flesh, a lunatic delivers a witty, chilling, disturbingly sane argument in favor of eating the rich.. **184 pages $11**

BB-109 **"Starfish Girl" Athena Villaverde**—In a post-apocalyptic underwater dome society, a girl with a starfish growing from her head and an assassin with sea anenome hair are on the run from a gang of mutant fish men. **160 pages $11**

BB-110 **"Lick Your Neighbor" Chris Genoa**—Mutant ninjas, a talking whale, kung fu masters, maniacal pilgrims, and an alcoholic clown populate Chris Genoa's surreal, darkly comical and unnerving reimagining of the first Thanksgiving. **303 pages $13**

BB-111 **"Night of the Assholes" Kevin L. Donihe**—A plague of assholes is infecting the countryside. Normal everyday people are transforming into jerks, snobs, dicks, and douchebags. And they all have only one purpose: to make your life a living hell.. **192 pages $11**

BB-112 **"Jimmy Plush, Teddy Bear Detective" Garrett Cook**—Hardboiled cases of a private detective trapped within a teddy bear body. **180 pages $11**

BB-113 **"The Deadheart Shelters" Forrest Armstrong**—The hip hop lovechild of William Burroughs and Dali... **144 pages $11**

BB-114 **"Eyeballs Growing All Over Me... Again" Tony Raugh**—Absurd, surreal, playful, dream-like, whimsical, and a lot of fun to read. **144 pages $11**

BB-115 "Whargoul" Dave Brockie — From the killing grounds of Stalingrad to the death camps of the holocaust. From torture chambers in Iraq to race riots in the United States, the Whargoul was there, killing and raping. **244 pages $12**

BB-116 "By the Time We Leave Here, We'll Be Friends" J. David Osborne — A David Lynchian nightmare set in a Russian gulag, where its prisoners, guards, traitors, soldiers, lovers, and demons fight for survival and their own rapidly deteriorating humanity. **168 pages $11**

BB-117 "Christmas on Crack" edited by Carlton Mellick III — Perverted Christmas Tales for the whole family! . . . as long as every member of your family is over the age of 18. **168 pages $11**

BB-118 "Crab Town" Carlton Mellick III — Radiation fetishists, balloon people, mutant crabs, sail-bike road warriors, and a love affair between a woman and an H-Bomb. This is one mean asshole of a city. Welcome to Crab Town. **100 pages $8**

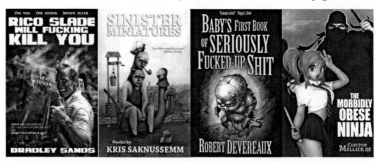

BB-119 "Rico Slade Will Fucking Kill You" Bradley Sands — Rico Slade is an action hero. Rico Slade can rip out a throat with his bare hands. Rico Slade's favorite food is the honey-roasted peanut. Rico Slade will fucking kill everyone. A novel. **122 pages $8**

BB-120 "Sinister Miniatures" Kris Saknussemm — The definitive collection of short fiction by Kris Saknussemm, confirming that he is one of the best, most daring writers of the weird to emerge in the twenty-first century. **180 pages $11**

BB-121 "Baby's First Book of Seriously Fucked up Shit" Robert Devereaux — Ten stories of the strange, the gross, and the just plain fucked up from one of the most original voices in horror. **176 pages $11**

BB-122 "The Morbidly Obese Ninja" Carlton Mellick III — These days, if you want to run a successful company . . . you're going to need a lot of ninjas. **92 pages $8**

BB-123 **"Abortion Arcade" Cameron Pierce** — An intoxicating blend of body horror and midnight movie madness, reminiscent of early David Lynch and the splatterpunks at their most sublime. **172 pages $11**

BB-124 **"Black Hole Blues" Patrick Wensink** — A hilarious double helix of country music and physics. **196 pages $11**

BB-125 **"Barbarian Beast Bitches of the Badlands" Carlton Mellick III** — Three prequels and sequels to *Warrior Wolf Women of the Wasteland*. **284 pages $13**

BB-126 **"The Traveling Dildo Salesman" Kevin L. Donihe** — A nightmare comedy about destiny, faith, and sex toys. Also featuring Donihe's most lurid and infamous short stories: *Milky Agitation, Two-Way Santa, The Helen Mower, Living Room Zombies,* and *Revenge of the Living Masturbation Rag*. **108 pages $8**

BB-127 **"Metamorphosis Blues" Bruce Taylor** — Enter a land of love beasts, intergalactic cowboys, and rock 'n roll. A land where Sears Catalogs are doorways to insanity and men keep mysterious black boxes. Welcome to the monstrous mind of Mr. Magic Realism. **136 pages $11**

BB-128 **"The Driver's Guide to Hitting Pedestrians" Andersen Prunty** — A pocket guide to the twenty-three most painful things in life, written by the most well-adjusted man in the universe. **108 pages $8**

BB-129 **"Island of the Super People" Kevin Shamel** — Four students and their anthropology professor journey to a remote island to study its indigenous population. But this is no ordinary native culture. They're super heroes and villains with flesh costumes and outlandish abilities like self-detonation, musical eyelashes, and microwave hands. **194 pages $11**

BB-130 **"Fantastic Orgy" Carlton Mellick III** — Shark Sex, mutant cats, and strange sexually transmitted diseases. Featuring the stories: *Candy-coated, Ear Cat, Fantastic Orgy, City Hobgoblins,* and *Porno in August*. **136 pages $9**

BB-131 **"Cripple Wolf" Jeff Burk** — Part man. Part wolf. 100% crippled. Also including *Punk Rock Nursing Home, Adrift with Space Badgers, Cook for Your Life, Just Another Day in the Park, Frosty and the Full Monty,* and *House of Cats.* **152 pages $10**

BB-132 **"I Knocked Up Satan's Daughter" Carlton Mellick III** — An adorable, violent, fantastical love story. A romantic comedy for the bizarro fiction reader. **152 pages $10**

BB-133 **"A Town Called Suckhole" David W. Barbee** — Far into the future, in the nuclear bowels of post-apocalyptic Dixie, there is a town. A town of derelict mobile homes, ancient junk, and mutant wildlife. A town of slack jawed rednecks who bask in the splendors of moonshine and mud boggin'. A town dedicated to the bloody and demented legacy of the Old South. A town called Suckhole. **144 pages $10**

BB-134 **"Cthulhu Comes to the Vampire Kingdom" Cameron Pierce** — What you'd get if H. P. Lovecraft wrote a Tim Burton animated film. **148 pages $11**

BB-135 **"I am Genghis Cum" Violet LeVoit** — From the savage Arctic tundra to post-partum mutations to your missing daughter's unmarked grave, join visionary madwoman Violet LeVoit in this non-stop eight-story onslaught of full-tilt Bizarro punk lit thrills. **124 pages $9**

BB-136 **"Haunt" Laura Lee Bahr** — A tripping-balls Los Angeles noir, where a mysterious dame drags you through a time-warping Bizarro hall of mirrors. **316 pages $13**

BB-137 **"Amazing Stories of the Flying Spaghetti Monster" edited by Cameron Pierce** — Like an all-spaghetti evening of Adult Swim, the Flying Spaghetti Monster will show you the many realms of His Noodly Appendage. Learn of those who worship him and the lives he touches in distant, mysterious ways. **228 pages $12**

BB-138 **"Wave of Mutilation" Douglas Lain** — A dream-pop exploration of modern architecture and the American identity, *Wave of Mutilation* is a Zen finger trap for the 21st century. **100 pages $8**

BB-139 **"Hooray for Death!" Mykle Hansen** — Famous Author Mykle Hansen draws unconventional humor from deaths tiny and large, and invites you to laugh while you can. **128 pages $10**

BB-140 **"Hypno-hog's Moonshine Monster Jamboree" Andrew Goldfarb** — Hicks, Hogs, Horror! Goldfarb is back with another strange illustrated tale of backwoods weirdness. **120 pages $9**

BB-141 **"Broken Piano For President" Patrick Wensink** — A comic masterpiece about the fast food industry, booze, and the necessity to choose happiness over work and security. **372 pages $15**

BB-142 **"Please Do Not Shoot Me in the Face" Bradley Sands** — A novel in three parts, *Please Do Not Shoot Me in the Face: A Novel*, is the story of one boy detective, the worst ninja in the world, and the great American fast food wars. It is a novel of loss, destruction, and--incredibly--genuine hope. **224 pages $12**

BB-143 **"Santa Steps Out" Robert Devereaux** — Sex, Death, and Santa Claus ... The ultimate erotic Christmas story is back. **294 pages $13**

BB-144 **"Santa Conquers the Homophobes" Robert Devereaux** — "I wish I could hope to ever attain one-thousandth the perversity of Robert Devereaux's toenail clippings." - Poppy Z. Brite **316 pages $13**

BB-145 **"We Live Inside You" Jeremy Robert Johnson** — "Jeremy Robert Johnson is dancing to a way different drummer. He loves language, he loves the edge, and he loves us people. These stories have range and style and wit. This is entertainment... and literature."- Jack Ketchum **188 pages $11**

BB-146 **"Clockwork Girl" Athena Villaverde** — Urban fairy tales for the weird girl in all of us. Like a combination of Francesca Lia Block, Charles de Lint, Kathe Koja, Tim Burton, and Hayao Miyazaki, her stories are cute, kinky, edgy, magical, provocative, and strange, full of poetic imagery and vicious sexuality. **160 pages $10**

BB-147 "Armadillo Fists" Carlton Mellick III — A weird-as-hell gangster story set in a world where people drive giant mechanical dinosaurs instead of cars. **168 pages $11**

BB-148 "Gargoyle Girls of Spider Island" Cameron Pierce — Four college seniors venture out into open waters for the tropical party weekend of a lifetime. Instead of a teenage sex fantasy, they find themselves in a nightmare of pirates, sharks, and sex-crazed monsters. **100 pages $8**

BB-149 "The Handsome Squirm" by Carlton Mellick III — Like Franz Kafka's *The Trial* meets an erotic body horror version of *The Blob*. **158 pages $11**

BB-150 "Tentacle Death Trip" Jordan Krall — It's *Death Race 2000* meets H. P. Lovecraft in bizarro author Jordan Krall's best and most suspenseful work to date. **224 pages $12**

The Obese Nick Antosca

HEVIN DONIHE

BB-151 "The Obese" Nick Antosca — Like Alfred Hitchcock's *The Birds*... but with obese people. **108 pages $10**

BB-152 "All-Monster Action!" Cody Goodfellow — The world gave him a blank check and a demand: Create giant monsters to fight our wars. But Dr. Otaku was not satisfied with mere chaos and mass destruction.... **216 pages $12**

BB-153 "Ugly Heaven" Carlton Mellick III — Heaven is no longer a paradise. It was once a blissful utopia full of wonders far beyond human comprehension. But the afterlife is now in ruins. It has become an ugly, lonely wasteland populated by strange monstrous beasts, masturbating angels, and sad man-like beings wallowing in the remains of the once-great Kingdom of God. **106 pages $8**

BB-154 "Space Walrus" Kevin L. Donihe — Walter is supposed to go where no walrus has ever gone before, but all this astronaut walrus really wants is to take it easy on the intense training, escape the chimpanzee bullies, and win the love of his human trainer Dr. Stephanie. **160 pages $11**

BB-155 **"Unicorn Battle Squad" Kirsten Alene** — Mutant unicorns. A palace with a thousand human legs. The most powerful army on the planet. **192 pages $11**

BB-156 **"Kill Ball" Carlton Mellick III** — In a city where all humans live inside of plastic bubbles, exotic dancers are being murdered in the rubbery streets by a mysterious stalker known only as Kill Ball. **134 pages $10**

BB-157 **"Die You Doughnut Bastards" Cameron Pierce** — The bacon storm is rolling in. We hear the grease and sugar beat against the roof and windows. The doughnut people are attacking. We press close together, forgetting for a moment that we hate each other. **196 pages $11**

BB-158 **"Tumor Fruit" Carlton Mellick III** — Eight desperate castaways find themselves stranded on a mysterious deserted island. They are surrounded by poisonous blue plants and an ocean made of acid. Ravenous creatures lurk in the toxic jungle. The ghostly sound of crying babies can be heard on the wind. **310 pages $13**

BB-159 **"Thunderpussy" David W. Barbee** — When it comes to high-tech global espionage, only one man has the balls to save humanity from the world's most powerful bastards. He's Declan Magpie Bruce, Agent 00X. **136 pages $11**

BB-160 **"Papier Mâché Jesus" Kevin L. Donihe** — Donihe's surreal wit and beautiful mind-bending imagination is on full display with stories such as All Children Go to Hell, Happiness is a Warm Gun, and Swimming in Endless Night. **154 pages $11**

BB-161 **"Cuddly Holocaust" Carlton Mellick III** — The war between humans and toys has come to an end. The toys won. **172 pages $11**

BB-162 **"Hammer Wives" Carlton Mellick III** — Fish-eyed mutants, oceans of insects, and flesh-eating women with hammers for heads. Hammer Wives collects six of his most popular novelettes and short stories. **152 pages $10**

CPSIA information can be obtained at www.ICGtesting.com
Printed in the USA
BVOW03s1455190114

342302BV00001B/10/P